PUFFIN

Bernard's Watch

Andrew Norriss was born in 1947, went to Trinity College, Dublin, and then became a school teacher because a woman called Mrs Morrison told him to. In 1982, another woman told him he should be a writer, so he did that instead, partly because of the money, but mostly because it means you can watch movies in the afternoon.

He lives in a thatched cottage in a little Hampshire village with a loving wife and two wonderful children, and life would be pretty near perfect if he could just get rid of the moles on the lawn, and his son didn't leave marmalade dribbling down the side of the jar so that it stuck on your fingers when you picked it up in the morning.

Books by Andrew Norriss

**AQUILA
BERNARD'S WATCH
MATT'S MILLION
THE TOUCHSTONE**

ANDREW NORRISS

BERNARD'S WATCH

PUFFIN

For Johnny

PUFFIN BOOKS

Published by the Penguin Group
Penguin Books Ltd, 80 Strand, London WC2R 0RL, England
Penguin Group (USA), Inc., 375 Hudson Street, New York, New York 10014, USA
Penguin Books Australia Ltd, 250 Camberwell Road, Camberwell, Victoria 3124, Australia
Penguin Books Canada Ltd, 10 Alcorn Avenue, Toronto, Ontario, Canada M4V 3B2
Penguin Books India (P) Ltd, 11 Community Centre, Panchsheel Park, New Delhi – 110 017, India
Penguin Group (NZ), cnr Airborne and Rosedale Roads, Albany, Auckland 1310, New Zealand
Penguin Books (South Africa) (Pty) Ltd, 24 Sturdee Avenue, Rosebank 2196, South Africa

Penguin Books Ltd, Registered Offices: 80 Strand, London WC2R 0RL, England

www.penguin.com

First published 1999
This edition published 2001
4

Copyright © Andrew Norriss, 1999
All rights reserved

The moral right of the author has been asserted

Set in Plantin

Made and printed in England by Clays Ltd, St Ives plc

Except in the United States of America, this book is sold subject to the condition
that it shall not, by way of trade or otherwise, be lent, re-sold, hired out, or otherwise
circulated without the publisher's prior consent in any form of binding or cover
other than that in which it is published and without a similar condition
including this condition being imposed on the subsequent purchaser

British Library Cataloguing in Publication Data
A CIP catalogue record for this book is available from the British Library

ISBN 0-141-30896-6

CONTENTS

1	GIVEN TIME	1
2	STILL TIME	9
3	TAKING TIME	20
4	TIME TRAVEL	32
5	VISITING TIME	44
6	SAVING TIME	56
7	TIME SHARE	68
8	FREE TIME	79
9	TIME OUT	93
10	LOST TIME	105
11	OUT OF TIME	116
12	STARTING TIME	126

Chapter One
GIVEN TIME

Bernard's aunt gave him the watch at a little after two o'clock on a Thursday afternoon in early February. Later, he would sometimes wonder why his aunt chose to give it to him at that particular time or, indeed, why she chose to give it to him at all, instead of to somebody else. But whatever the reason, he was always extremely grateful to her. It was the perfect present at the time because, at the time, time was exactly what he needed.

Strictly speaking, she was not Bernard's aunt, but his great-aunt. She was the sister of his mother's mother and her full name was Mrs Beatrice Anne Temperley, but everyone called her Aunt Bee.

She was a short woman with short grey hair, who walked with the help of a short stick, and when she saw Bernard standing on the pavement at the end of her garden, she knew immediately that something was wrong. Apart from the worried look on his face, there was the fact that he wasn't wearing any trousers.

She came out of her house and called to him from the top of the steps.

'Bernard? Is everything all right?'

'Hello, Auntie!' Bernard gave her a wave.

'You're not wearing any trousers.'

'No.' Bernard nodded. 'No, that's right.'

'And aren't you supposed to be in school?'

'Yes,' Bernard nodded again. 'Yes, I am.'

Aunt Bee beckoned him towards the house. 'I think you'd better come in and tell me what's happened.'

With a slight feeling of relief, Bernard made his way through the gate and up the steps into the house. If you had a problem, it was always a good idea to share it with Aunt Bee. He did not know why but, when Aunt Bee took charge of them, problems had a habit of fading away like wrinkles under a steam iron. Though even she, Bernard thought, was going to find it difficult to get him out of this one.

'You can leave that in the hall –' she pointed to the bag Bernard carried on his shoulder – 'and then come on through.'

The football bag, Bernard thought as he put it on the floor by the front door before following his aunt into what she called the drawing room. That was what had started all the trouble.

The football bag.

Until Miss Picot stood up in the dining room at lunchtime, Bernard had quite forgotten that football practice had been changed to Thursdays. Even then, as she reminded everyone in Year 7 that they had to be changed and out on the field by ten minutes past two, he was not worried until Karen, sitting beside him, pointed out that he had not brought his football things to school that morning.

Bernard was rather surprised, not at the fact that he had forgotten his football things – that happened quite often – but that Karen had spoken to him. She was a quiet girl who had only joined the school that term and very rarely spoke to anyone.

'Didn't I?' he said. 'Are you sure?'

Karen nodded. 'You brought your school bag and coat, but no football stuff.' She paused and then added, 'You're going to get into trouble, aren't you?'

'Yes,' said Bernard. 'Thank you.'

Trouble from Miss Picot was something most people tried to avoid. The teacher was a big woman, nearly seven feet tall, who had once played international rugby for Sweden and, although Bernard was not exactly frightened of her, he preferred to avoid making her angry if he could. He decided the simplest thing would to be to go home and get his football things.

Leaving school premises without permission was, of course, strictly forbidden, but Bernard's house was only two hundred metres down the road. As long as no one saw him leave the playground, he thought, he could run home, let himself into the house with the front-door key hidden under the stone in the garden, collect his football kit and be back at school in a matter of minutes. No one need ever know.

Unfortunately, it had all taken a bit longer than he

had expected. He got out of the playground without any difficulty, got home, let himself into the house with the spare key and eventually found his football kit hanging behind the pantry door in the kitchen. However, as he swung the bag over his shoulder, he knocked over a bottle of milk that had been left with all the breakfast things on the table.

He put down the bag, cleared up most of the broken glass, picked up his bag again, hurried down the hall and ran out of the front door. Then, as he banged it closed behind him and set off down the steps, he found he had shut part of his right trouser leg in the door.

He tried to pull himself free. He tried very hard, but however much he pulled, the leg of his trousers stayed firmly trapped. He reached into his pocket for the key to open the door . . . and remembered he had left it on the kitchen table when he went to clear up the broken bottle. He stood there for some minutes until, in the end, he did the only thing he could think of.

He took off his trousers and left them there, stuck in the door.

He went round to the back of the house to see if he could climb in through a window, either to get the key or another pair of trousers, but all the windows were closed. In the end, it seemed the only thing left to do was to go and see his aunt.

Walking along the street without any trousers was a little embarrassing but, fortunately, his coat came down to his knees and it was not far. His aunt's house was next door to the school and he was about to turn into her gate when he saw Mr Tree appear in the playground ahead of him, ringing the bell to call everyone back into school.

It was the end of the lunch break. Bernard was outside school grounds. He had no trousers and he was, he now realized, in far worse trouble than if he had simply gone to Miss Picot in the first place and told her he had forgotten his football bag.

He was still standing there, wondering what to do, when Aunt Bee saw him and called out to ask if everything was all right.

'I'll tell you what you can do,' she said, when Bernard finished explaining what had happened.

She was sitting at one end of a large leather sofa in the drawing room, while Bernard sat on a matching sofa on the other side of the fireplace.

'You can borrow this.' She unclipped a pocket watch from the chain that attached it to a buttonhole in her blouse. 'But, please, make sure you look after it carefully.'

Bernard took the watch. He had seen it many times before, his aunt wore it all the time, but he had never held it. In most respects, it was an ordinary pocket watch with a gold case and a glass circle in the front, which allowed you to see the hands and the numbers on the face beneath. There were three hands – one for the hours, one for the minutes and a third, ticking out the seconds. The time was three minutes past two.

At the top of the watch was a button. Not a

winder, as you would expect to find, but a cylindrical button of smooth gold like the one you sometimes get on the end of a ballpoint pen and that you click in and out when you want to write. The whole thing felt heavy and there was an odd feeling of resistance as he took it, as if it wanted to stay where it was and not be pulled through the air.

'I was going to let you try it out some time soon anyway.' Aunt Bee smiled at him. 'But now seems as good a time as any.'

'You're lending this to me?' Bernard looked up from examining the watch. 'What for?'

'A good question.' Aunt Bee nodded approvingly. 'And, in a sense, what it's for is the only question worth asking, but not the one you need to worry about at the moment. What you want to know is what it *does*.'

'Do I?' Bernard looked at the watch again and at the button at the top. 'Why?'

'The watch does rather more than tell the time.' Aunt Bee leaned forward and lowered her voice as she spoke. 'It's what you might call . . . a stop watch.' She pointed at the button at the top. 'If you press that, you'll find out why. You see, this –'

Bernard pressed the button and the watch stopped. Then he looked up and saw his aunt had stopped as well.

Not just stopped talking.

Stopped.

'Auntie?' Bernard reached out and touched her arm. 'Auntie, are you all right?'

The old woman did not reply. Nor did she move, or speak, or breathe and Bernard's first thought was that, in mid-sentence, her finger poised in the air, she had quite suddenly died. Almost without thinking he ran out to the front door, flung it open and shouted 'Help! Please! Somebody, help!' at the top of his voice.

But it was like a bad dream. However loudly he shouted, no sound came out of his mouth. In fact, no sound came from anywhere. Since Bernard had pressed the button on the watch, the world had become totally silent.

And still.

In rising panic, as he gazed up and down the road in front of the house, Bernard saw that everything had stopped. In the garden opposite, the leaves blown up by the wind hung in the air like fruit in a jelly. Down the road a man was frozen in the act of mounting his bicycle. Along the pavement, a woman pushing a small child in a buggy was standing, one foot motionless in front of the other, as still as a statue. It was as if the whole world were a giant video and someone had pressed the pause button.

Slowly, Bernard turned round and went back into the house. In the living room, he stood for some seconds in front of his aunt, and then did the only thing he could think of doing. He sat down on the sofa and pressed the button on the watch again.

'– is a watch that can stop time. But don't be frightened. Any time you want it to start again, you simply press the button.' Aunt Beatrice looked at

Bernard. 'Go on. Try it!'

'I just did,' said Bernard, feeling a little dazed.

'Of course,' his Aunt smiled. 'I keep forgetting what it's like when someone else has it. Well?'

'It was . . . it was amazing.' Bernard was still staring at the watch in his hand. 'But why . . . I mean, how . . . What . . . What happened?'

'I told you. The watch stops time.' Aunt Bee stood up. 'Now, explanations later. The important thing is to get you back to school before anyone notices you're not there. After all, you don't want to be late, do you?'

'But I'm already late,' said Bernard.

Aunt Bee rested a hand on his shoulder. 'You've got the watch, Bernard,' she said gently. 'You have to understand that, while you've got that, you don't have to be late for anything. Ever.'

Chapter Two
STILL TIME

It took a bit of getting used to. As he walked through the school gates, Bernard stepped carefully over a small dog, frozen in the act of lifting its leg against one of the pillars. On the far side of the playground, Mr Wickerstaffe, the caretaker, was in the middle of emptying a dustpan into the one of the bins at the side of the school while two sparrows, chasing each other round the climbing frame, were low enough in their flight for Bernard to actually reach up and touch their wings.

He had already been home and used the key Aunt Bee had given him to retrieve his trousers from the front door. Now he made his way into the school and along the corridor to the changing rooms.

On either side, he passed classrooms where children and teachers sat, noiseless and unmoving, at their desks. In the hall, the school orchestra with Mr Tree conducting and Karen playing her cello, were frozen in their seats. And when he got to the changing room, he found Miss Picot standing stock still in the doorway with her mouth wide open as if she was in the middle of telling someone off.

His aunt had warned Bernard that it was dangerous to start time again when someone might be watching. If he pressed the button on the watch while standing in front of Miss Picot, for instance, it would seem to the teacher that he had appeared out of thin air. From her point of view, an empty space would suddenly be filled by an eleven-year-old boy and it was, Aunt Bee had explained, the sort of experience that not only led to embarrassing questions, but gave people heart attacks.

The changing room was L-shaped and Bernard made his way past the other children getting changed to a place round the corner, out of sight. He dropped his bag on the bench and was about to pull off his sweater, when he noticed another interesting effect of being in frozen time. His bag, when he let go of it, did not fall on to the bench. Falling is something that takes time and, since time had stopped, his bag stayed exactly where it was when he let go of it. His sweater, when he pulled it over his head, hung in the air as if there were still an invisible body inside it. And when he tried to hang it up, it streamed out from the hook like a windsock, until he pulled it down into position.

It made changing a little more complicated than usual. The sleeves of his football shirt were never quite where his arms expected them to be and doing up his football boots with laces that only moved when you moved them was tricky. But when Bernard had finally finished, he put the watch carefully in the pocket of his football shorts and pressed the button.

The noise was instantaneous and the loudest voice was Miss Picot's, calling out over the hubbub, '. . . must know where he is! Didn't anyone see him during the lunch break? Anyone at all?'

'He's over here,' said a boy who had come round the corner and seen Bernard sitting on the bench. A moment later, Miss Picot was standing in front of him, staring down from her imposing height, a deep frown on her face.

'Bernard? What are you doing round here?'

Bernard's thumb rested on the button of the watch in his pocket. He found the feel of it somehow reassuring.

'I've been asking where you were for the last three minutes.' Miss Picot was still frowning. 'Didn't you hear?'

Before Bernard could answer, a football sailed over the coat rack from the other side of the changing room. It was heading, with some speed, for the side of Miss Picot's face. Bernard's thumb pressed down on the button of the watch.

The ball froze in mid-air, along with everything else, and Bernard reached out and caught it. There was no point letting anything happen to make Miss Picot angrier than she already was. Holding the ball firmly to his chest, he started time again.

A boy's head appeared above the coat rack.

'Sorry,' he said sheepishly. 'I was practising a drop kick and it slipped.'

To Bernard's surprise, Miss Picot did not reply. Normally, messing around with a ball in the changing room would have resulted in some very sharp words, but she ignored the boy completely. Instead, she looked thoughtfully at Bernard before reaching out to take the ball from his hands.

'I'm sorry I didn't hear you,' said Bernard. 'I was busy getting changed.'

'Yes . . .' The frown on Miss Picot's face had disappeared.

'You caught this very quickly,' she said, bouncing the football on the ground. 'Have you ever thought of playing in goal?'

Bernard was not a boy who had ever been particularly good at sport, but that afternoon he played what Miss Picot called an inspired game in goal.

From Bernard's point of view, it was all very simple. A few minutes into the game, when a boy called Louis Hugh-Jones began racing towards him with the ball, Bernard found his thumb moving automatically to the watch in his pocket. It was poised over the button when Louis, who was about ten metres from the goal, thumped the ball as hard as he could . . .

. . . and time stopped.

In the silence, Bernard looked at the football poised in the air and calculated that it was heading for the top right hand corner of the goalmouth behind him. It was too high for him to be sure of catching it, and he decided the simplest thing would be to punch it over the bar. In frozen time, he took two paces to his right, pressed the watch with one hand to restart time, and used the other to punch the ball with his fist.

'Well done! Good save!' Miss Picot came bounding up the field, her long blonde hair billowing behind her, while Louis stared at Bernard in open-mouthed astonishment.

When the corner was taken and another boy headed the ball towards the goal, Bernard did the same thing again. He stopped time, worked out where the ball was going, moved to the best position to stop it, and stopped it. He was beginning to enjoy himself and, in the course of the next half hour, produced seven quite dramatic saves and stopped a penalty. Miss Picot was delighted.

'Is there any chance you could play for us on Saturday?' she asked, as they left the field at the end of the practice.

'You mean in the team?' Bernard was rather taken aback at the idea.

'Certainly in the team.' Miss Picot beamed down at him. 'It's a home match. Starts at eleven. Can you do it?'

Bernard had never been in a school team for anything, but the more he thought about it, the more he found he liked the idea. He was about to say so, when he remembered that on Saturday he would not have the watch. His aunt had only lent it to him for the afternoon.

'I'd like to,' he said eventually. 'But I'm not sure I'll have the time.'

'Well, see if you can.' Miss Picot pushed open the door to the school building. 'Believe me, we need someone like you.'

She watched him walk down the corridor to the changing room with considerable satisfaction. The school football team had been shaping up rather well recently, but the one thing the squad had been missing was a decent goalkeeper. And, as soon as she had seen Bernard catch that ball in the changing rooms, she had known there was no need to look any further.

In all her years as a sportswoman and teacher, she had never seen anyone move so *fast*.

At half-past three, Bernard came out of school and walked round to his aunt's house. He went there every day after lessons, staying with his aunt until his father called in to pick him up on the way back from work. Aunt Bee was the one who gave him his tea and made sure that he did his homework.

Walking up the steps to her front door, he could see his aunt sitting at her desk in the window, waving at him to come straight in. The front door was never locked, although Mrs Donaldson, the woman who came in the mornings to do the cleaning, always said how unsafe it was and that one day someone was going to come in and steal everything.

'Well? How was it?' Aunt Bee swivelled round in her chair as Bernard came in to the drawing room.

'It was incredible!' said Bernard. 'Honestly, you wouldn't believe it, I . . .'

He stopped. He had just noticed that Aunt Bee had another watch, exactly like the one in his pocket, on the chain hanging from her blouse.

'You've got *two* of them?'

'What?' Aunt Bee realized what he meant and shook her head. 'Oh no! No, no, no! This one is a copy. It's useful sometimes to let people think that I . . .' She gestured Bernard to a chair. 'But never mind that now, I want to know what you've been doing. Come on. Tell me all about it.'

Bernard sat down and told her everything that had happened. He told her about not getting into trouble for being late (because no one knew that he *had* been), about what had happened with the football in the changing room and about being in goal. Aunt Bee nodded and smiled as she listened.

'Good,' she said, when he finished. 'I'm glad you enjoyed yourself.'

'It was amazing.' Bernard felt a slight twinge of regret as he passed over the watch. 'Where did you get it from?'

'Well, I was given it. By him.' Aunt Bee pointed to a picture on the desk. It was a black-and-white photograph in a silver frame of a young man with crinkly dark hair and a moustache, standing on top of a mountain.

'He was my husband. Philip.'

Bernard picked up the photo to look at it more closely.

'And where did he get it?'

'He was given it by his grandfather.' Aunt Bee was carefully cleaning the face of the watch with a tissue as she spoke. 'But where he got it from, we never knew. Unfortunately, at the time he gave the watch to Philip, he had recently been the victim of a stroke and was unable to speak. He died two weeks later.'

'Without telling you anything?'

'I'm afraid so. We searched through all his papers after the funeral, but there was nothing to show where or when he found the watch. He'd travelled all over the world – Africa, South America, the Far East – he could have found it anywhere. We searched his house, read his diaries, talked to his friends . . . but nothing.'

Aunt Bee placed the watch carefully on her desk and turned to Bernard.

'Would you like to borrow it for a bit longer?'

There was nothing in the world that Bernard wanted more and he said so.

Aunt Bee pushed the watch towards him. 'You'll have to give it back to me tomorrow though. After school again. Is that all right?'

'Great.' Bernard nodded happily.

'Well, you'd better have something to eat and drink, and do your homework.' His aunt got up and led Bernard over to the sofa. 'And then I'll go over some of the things you'll need to watch out for.'

On the table between the sofas was a plate of sandwiches and a large glass of lemonade.

'I told you how important it was not to tell anyone about it, didn't I?'

'Yes.' Bernard took a sip of the lemonade. It had an odd taste, but that was probably because his aunt made it herself with real lemons.

'There are several other things I ought to warn you about,' Aunt Bee continued. 'Like being careful in the rain, and not going to the toilet in frozen time. But homework first, I think.'

'Homework's already done.' Bernard was holding the watch in one hand and an exercise book in the other.

Aunt Bee picked up the exercise book and looked at the two carefully written pages Bernard had done for Miss Picot, describing what it felt like to be a seagull trapped in an oil slick.

'You did this just now?'

'Homework doesn't take any time at all.' Bernard smiled happily. 'Not when you've got the watch. So why do I have to be careful in the rain?'

While Aunt Bee explained to Bernard how the water built up in front of your face and got in your nose while walking in frozen time when it was raining, she could not help but notice how her great-nephew was already changing.

He was not aware of it himself, but there was an air about him as he sat back on the sofa, a relaxed confidence that came, she knew, to anyone who had the watch. It was one of the results of knowing you had as much time as you needed to do anything that needed doing. You stopped worrying. About anything. Bernard had barely had the watch for two hours, but already she could see the difference.

'And what about going to the toilet?' he asked, when she had finished explaining about the rain. 'Why don't I do that?'

'Ah, the toilet!' Aunt Bee sighed. 'Well, I won't go into the details if you don't mind. But take my word, it . . . it gets very messy.'

Mr Beasley, Bernard's father, did not notice anything different about his son when he arrived just after seven, but that was possibly because he was still thinking about his work.

Mr Beasley owned a transport company with twenty-three articulated lorries that carried refrigerated goods all over Europe. It was a highly successful and expanding business, but it had only become that way because Mr Beasley, who had founded it, gave it long hours and careful management.

As he sat with Bernard in the kitchen that evening, eating the fish and chips he had bought on the way home, he spent most of the time making a series of business phone calls. And when they finished, Bernard put the breakfast dishes in the washer while Mr Beasley went into the front room, which he used as an office, to do some more work.

When he came up to say goodnight, however, he noticed the watch on Bernard's bedside table and asked where he had got it.

'Aunt Bee lent it to me.' Bernard picked up the watch and held it.

'Lent it to you? What for?'

'She thought it might help me,' said Bernard, 'to have the time.'

'Well, for goodness sake look after it.' Mr Beasley was already heading for the door. 'It looks as if it might be quite valuable.'

He was halfway down the stairs when he remembered that he had meant to ask Bernard about the broken milk bottle in the waste bin. It was odd. He remembered the bottle had definitely been on the table when they left in the morning but, when they came back, he had found it in pieces in the bin . . .

Mr Beasley hesitated, wondering if he should go back upstairs and see if Bernard could explain it, but decided in the end not to bother. It wasn't very important after all, and questions might set Bernard off worrying again. He did a lot of worrying. And, Mr Beasley thought, he still had a great deal of work to do.

So he carried on down the stairs to get on with it.

Chapter Three
TAKING TIME

The next morning, when Bernard found he had slept through the alarm and there was only a quarter of an hour to get dressed, have breakfast and be ready for school, he simply reached out for the watch by his bed and pressed the button. There was nothing to worry about. If need be, he could be dressed and ready in no time at all.

Well, almost. Although he could get dressed in frozen time, he found cleaning his teeth and washing were easier without the watch. It helped to have water running out of the taps if you wanted to use soap or rinse your mouth of toothpaste and water did not run when time had stopped.

Eating a slow, leisurely breakfast, on the other hand, was no problem at all. Although Bernard needed real time to pour milk over his cereal (otherwise nothing came out of the bottle), he could take as long as he wanted to eat it. In fact, he took his toast and marmalade back to bed and finished the last chapter of his book there before eventually coming back downstairs to get his bag ready for school.

Mr Beasley was rather surprised to find Bernard in his school clothes, his bag at his feet and his hair neatly brushed, watching television when there were still ten minutes before he had to leave.

'What's happening then?' he asked, hastily gathering up the papers he would need for work that day and stuffing them into his briefcase.

Bernard gave a start. 'Happening? Where?'

'I was wondering why you were ready for school so early. Thought maybe there was something special happening.' Mr Beasley paused for a moment and a worried look crossed his face. 'I'm not missing another parents' day, am I?'

'Oh no. Nothing like that.' Bernard shook his head reassuringly. 'It's just a normal day.' He looked at the watch in his hand. 'Only I found I had some extra time this morning.'

Which was true, but not quite all of the truth. Bernard was, in fact, hoping that his day would be anything but normal. Lying in bed the night before, he had spent a good deal of time thinking of all the things he might do with the watch and, for a start, he was particularly looking forward to using it in Miss Picot's maths test.

Miss Picot was Bernard's form teacher and every Friday, after taking the register, she gave her class a test in mental arithmetic. She would call out a series of questions and the children had to work out the answers in their head. For Bernard, who was not particularly good at maths, the process had always been something of a trial.

Today, however, was different.

As soon as Miss Picot had asked her first question, which was 'What are seven fours plus two?', Bernard reached into the pocket of his trousers and pressed the button on his watch. In frozen time, he took out his tables book and looked up the answer to seven fours, which was twenty-eight, added two, which made thirty, and wrote the answer down before putting the book away and pressing the watch to start time again.

'Question two.' Miss Picot was speaking again almost at once. 'Nine multiplied by three, plus four.'

There were forty questions altogether and, when they swapped papers at the end to mark them, Bernard found he had got them all right. He was the only person in the class who had and Miss Picot could not have been more pleased. She had never found maths an easy subject to get across, but if someone like Bernard could make such a dramatic improvement after only a few weeks in her class, there was obviously nothing to worry about.

In the course of the morning, Bernard found his watch could help him in most subjects. In Geography, Mrs Lowes announced that they would be looking at Portugal and began by asking if anyone knew the name of its capital city.

Bernard had no idea at all, but thought it would

be easy enough to find out. There was a large map of the world on one wall of the classroom and he pressed the watch, got up, and went over to look at it. It took him a while to find Portugal and although it did not say which city was the capital, the writing on the word 'Lisbon' was darker and larger than any of the other cities.

He came back to his desk, sat down in his chair, pressed the watch, and put up his hand.

'Lisbon, miss?'

'Quite right.' Mrs Lowes smiled approvingly. 'And can anyone tell me anything about Portugal? How the people there earn their livings? What sort of things they produce?'

Bernard put his hand up.

'Yes, Bernard?'

'Wine, miss. Olive oil, sardines, textiles and pottery.'

Mrs Lowes was almost too astonished to speak. He was quite right. Indeed, this was exactly the answer written in the textbook, open on her desk. When she asked Bernard how he knew, he said he thought he had read it somewhere.

It seemed that Bernard had been doing a lot of reading. He knew what the Portuguese currency was (the escudo), the name of the country's most famous wine (port) and the size of its population (9.8 million).

In the history lesson that followed, Mr Bainbridge was equally astonished to discover that Bernard knew the names of all the British prime ministers in the last century. And in Science, with Mrs Lowes again, Bernard was the only one in the class to know the names and positions of the seven primary internal organs of the human body.

In the last lesson before lunch, feeling a little hungry, Bernard froze time and went into the staffroom where he found a tin of biscuits. He took two before walking into the kitchens, where he saw they were preparing a trifle for lunch. He helped himself to a portion and then had a drink of squash from a jug, using a straw. After that, feeling a little tired, he went to lie down on the bed in the sick room and fell asleep.

He had no idea how long he slept, because the clocks all said exactly the same time when he woke up as they had when he fell asleep, but he felt a lot better. For everyone else, of course, no time had passed at all, and Bernard happily pressed the watch again after rejoining his friends in class, and then astonished the French teacher by scoring a hundred per cent in a vocabulary test.

There was one slightly alarming moment at the end of the day when Mr Tree, the head teacher, asked to see Bernard in his office. He said he had heard Bernard had done very well in the maths test that morning and wanted to know why he was suddenly doing so much better than before.

'You're quite sure –' he looked over his glasses at Bernard – 'that you found the answers to this test on your own?'

Bernard thought carefully and decided the one

thing you could definitely say was that he had been on his own when he found the answers to the test.

'Yes,' he said.

'In that case, perhaps you won't mind if I ask you a few questions myself.' Mr Tree got up from his chair and paced up and down the carpet for a moment. 'What are six fours, plus five?'

'Six fours . . .' Bernard murmured thoughtfully, and put a hand in his pocket and pressed the button on the watch.

His first thought was to go back to his classroom and get his tables book, but unfortunately Mr Tree was leaning against the door.

His next thought was to use the calculator from the headmaster's desk, but even before he picked it up and pressed the buttons, Bernard realized it was not going to work. Calculators are very fast, but they still take time to do their calculating. And time had stopped.

In the end, he realized he had no choice but to work out the answer on his own and, sitting at the headmaster's desk, he took a blank sheet of paper and cut it into squares with a pair of scissors. He arranged the squares of paper into six rows of four, and put five more squares in another row underneath. Then he counted the pieces of paper, counted them again to make sure he had not made a mistake, and sat back down in his chair and pressed the watch.

'Twenty-nine,' he said.

Mr Tree blinked. 'Quite right. Yes, indeed. What about nine threes, plus eight?'

Bernard furrowed his brow in thought as he

pressed the watch again. He had to cut up some more pieces of paper to do this one, but working out the answer was easy enough. He counted the rows of squares very carefully to make sure there was no mistake, and sat back in his chair.

'Thirty-five?' Bernard tried to put a little uncertainty into his voice. He didn't want it to sound as if the questions were too easy.

'Well done, again – and so fast!'

Mr Tree was delighted. In the course of the next twenty seconds he fired off three more questions, none of which caused Bernard much difficulty and each time his smile grew broader and his congratulations louder.

He was launching into a problem that involved subtracting three hundred and fifty from five hundred and twenty-seven, which had Bernard worried where he was going to find enough pieces of paper, when Miss Picot knocked at the door.

'I've just been going over some maths with young Bernard here.' Mr Tree brought her into the room. 'And you're quite right. A remarkably quick mind. Answered all my questions with no difficulty at all. The only thing that puzzles me –' he gazed down at Bernard as he spoke – 'is why he couldn't do it before?'

There was a pause, and Bernard suddenly realized he was supposed to provide some sort of an answer.

'Well . . .' he hesitated. 'Well . . . I suppose you could say I've been giving my school work a bit more time recently.'

'Excellent!' Mr Tree banged his fist on the desk. 'Excellent answer. Now . . .' He sat down. 'One more thing before you go. Miss Picot and I are hoping very much that you'll be able to play in the school football team tomorrow. Have you thought any more about it?'

'Bernard? Came top in maths?' Mrs Hewitt looked in some surprise at her daughter. 'Are you sure?'

The two of them were sitting at the table in the front room of Mrs Hewitt's basement flat, while Karen did her homework. Mrs Hewitt liked to supervise homework to make sure it was done properly and, when it was finished, she would listen while her daughter did her cello practice and then help with the project she was doing on The World's Biggest Bridges.

Mrs Hewitt took school work very seriously. As she often said, people who did not take school work seriously, however clever they were, could wind up with no qualifications, in dead-end jobs, marrying the first person who asked them simply because they couldn't think of anything better.

This was, in fact, what had happened to Mrs Hewitt, and she spoke on the subject with some feeling. She had left school when she was fifteen, got married a year later, been divorced before Karen was born two years after that, and now worked part time in a shop that sold greetings cards.

'You're sure he wasn't cheating or anything?' Mrs Hewitt was still puzzled by the news about Bernard.

'I mean, could he have copied the answers from someone else?'

Karen shook her head.

'Nobody else had all the right answers to copy. He was the only one who got full marks.'

Karen herself had made two mistakes in the test. She liked to make at least two mistakes in any test she took. She had found that being seen as too clever only led to difficulties and she had enough of those already.

'And they've moved him up to your table?' Mrs Hewitt frowned thoughtfully. She had met Bernard on several occasions and he had not given the impression of great intelligence. She was quite sure she had seen him, only the day before, running down the pavement at lunchtime with no trousers.

She stood up and walked over to the window. Maybe she had misjudged him. If Bernard was as clever as her daughter said, the two children might have something in common after all. She knew Karen was finding it difficult to settle in at the new school. She was not the sort of girl who made friends easily and there had been an unfortunate incident of bullying on the first day that Mr Tree had dealt with very promptly, but which hadn't helped.

Maybe, she thought, it would be a good idea to take the children out together somewhere and give them a chance to get to know each other. On Saturdays, she liked to take Karen somewhere educationally stimulating. Perhaps she could invite Bernard to come with them.

Yes, she decided. She would call on Mr Beasley the next day and see what he thought of the idea.

Bernard was sitting with his aunt in the conservatory at the back of her house, while she catalogued the contents of a jam jar full of moths. Aunt Bee was the Moth Officer for the County branch of the Butterfly Conservation Society and, three times a week, she set a moth trap in her garden and carefully recorded her finds in a notebook the following day. Bernard was not sure why his aunt found moths so appealing, but it was something she had been doing for many years.

While she worked, Bernard sat in a canvas chair eating a sandwich and telling her about his day. He had been a little concerned that Aunt Bee might not approve of using the watch to do well in a maths test, but she seemed to think it was an excellent idea. She laughed out loud when she heard how Bernard had been stuck in Mr Tree's office and had to cut up pieces of paper to work out answers to his questions.

'It was one of the first things I learnt with the watch,' she said, scooping an escaped moth into her hands and releasing it out of the window. 'That, with time, you can do all sorts of things you thought you couldn't. When I was a girl, there were so many things I thought I couldn't do. But when Philip gave me the watch, I realized all I usually needed was more time. It's all most of us usually need.'

'And there's always enough time with this, isn't there?' said Bernard.

He had been about to ask if he could be allowed

to keep the watch for another day, so that he could play in the football match, but at the last minute he changed his mind. It was one of those things, like asking someone for money, that he felt you should only do in an emergency.

Instead, he pushed the watch across the table.

'Thanks again for letting me borrow it, Auntie. It's been fantastic.'

'I'm glad it was fun.'

'Oh, it was more than fun . . .' Bernard searched for the words that might explain the way having the watch made him feel. It certainly *was* fun to be clever in class and good at football and to walk out of a lesson without anyone knowing, but having the watch was much more than that, though it wasn't easy to explain why.

'It's . . . it's like being set free, isn't it?' he said, eventually. 'Like someone has let you out of a prison.'

'Let out of a prison!' Aunt Bee smiled. 'Well, if it does something as important as that, perhaps you'd better keep it for a bit longer and bring it back to me tomorrow. All right?' Without waiting for Bernard to reply, she pointed to his glass on the table.

'Now drink up. I made that lemonade specially for you.'

Later, she walked Bernard to the front door and watched from the steps as he went off down the path to join his father waiting in the car by the pavement. He had the watch firmly clutched in his hand and he gave a last excited wave before getting in and disappearing up the road to his house.

As she turned to go back indoors, Aunt Bee's smile faded and she leaned more heavily on her stick.

She was very old, older than most people knew, and sometimes she felt it. She ought to have started this whole business sooner. She knew that now.

For Bernard had been wrong about one thing. He had said that, with the watch, you had enough time for anything, but unfortunately that was not true.

Watch or no watch, Aunt Bee knew that her own time was running out.

Chapter Four
TIME TRAVEL

Mr Beasley had just sat down to start filling in a form from the government, which required him to calculate the average number of hours per week that his drivers had been on the road during the previous year, when the front door bell rang.

Still clutching the form (which ran to seventy-four pages) he opened the door to find a neatly dressed woman standing on the step. She had neat blonde hair, a freshly ironed blouse tucked neatly into her skirt and he had the vague feeling he had seen her somewhere before.

'Mr Beasley? Alison. Alison Hewitt,' she held out a hand.

Mr Beasley shook it, uncomfortably conscious of the fact that he had not shaved that morning, that he was not wearing any socks, and that getting dressed had mostly involved pulling a sweater on, over his pyjamas.

'I hope you'll forgive my calling, but my daughter, Karen, and your son are in the same form at school. As I'm sure you know.'

'Ah . . .'

Mr Beasley now remembered who the woman was. She had moved into the basement flat next door soon after Christmas. He was about to ask if she would like to come in for a cup of coffee, when he remembered the kitchen still had yesterday's supper dishes as well as the remains of breakfast on the table and changed his mind.

'Yes, of course. What can I do for you?'

'I wondered if Bernard would like to come out this afternoon. Only I'm taking Karen to the Naval Heritage Museum at Portsmouth.'

'Oh!' Mr Beasley's face brightened. 'Well, that's very kind.'

'I thought, as they seemed to have a shared enthusiasm for maths, they might get on well together.'

Mr Beasley blinked. 'Maths?'

'It's Karen's favourite subject as well.' Mrs Hewitt smiled as she added. 'Between the two of us, I think she was a little put out when Bernard beat her in the test yesterday!'

Mr Beasley stared at her, his mouth open. 'Are you sure we're talking about the same person?'

Mrs Hewitt flushed. 'If he doesn't want to come, of course, I'll quite understand. But perhaps you'd pass on the invitation.'

'Yes. Yes, I will. In fact, I'll ask him now.'

Mr Beasley turned back into the house and was about to call up the stairs when he remembered something and came back to the front door.

'Well, I would ask him, but I think he's out at the moment.'

'Yes.' Mrs Hewitt nodded. 'Playing football. Karen's gone to watch. But she says the match finishes at twelve and we weren't thinking of leaving until after that, so it should be all right.'

Mr Beasley was staring at her with his mouth open again.

'Football? Bernard's playing football?'

'For the school team,' said Mrs Hewitt. 'Didn't you know? They found he had a bit of a flair for goalkeeping.'

As she returned to her flat, Mrs Hewitt wondered how anybody could not know that their son had come top in a test, or that they were in the school team for one of its sports. She usually had a certain fellow feeling for single parents. She knew how difficult it was to bring up a child on your own, but she thought Mr Beasley needed to do a serious update of his parenting skills.

Mr Beasley, meanwhile, returned to his front room and wondered why Bernard had not said anything about playing in a match that morning. Or maybe he had. He knew he didn't always listen when the lad was talking. The trouble was there were so many other things to do . . .

For a moment, Mr Beasley considered walking down to the playing field to see what was happening, but then he realized that would mean getting shaved and dressed and by the time he had done that, the game would probably be over.

And the form he was still holding had to be filled in by Monday. His company employed twenty-four drivers and he would have to go through their weekly work sheets for the last year, adding up how many hours driving they had done and then working out the average.

He stared at the piles of papers, files, dockets and invoices that covered the table, his desk and a good deal of the floor. His first problem, he thought, would be finding where he had put the worksheets . . .

Bernard was delighted to be invited out. These days, with his father usually working at the weekends and Aunt Bee almost entirely housebound since the trouble with her hip, a trip out was something of a novelty.

The football match that morning had gone very well. The school had won by two goals to nothing. Both goals had been scored by Louis Hugh-Jones, the team captain and remarkably good striker, but most people seemed to think that it was Bernard's impenetrable defence, particularly in the early stages of the game, that had guaranteed the win. A good many of them came up afterwards to congratulate him, and the teacher in charge of the other team even asked Bernard if he had ever thought of changing schools.

And now he was in the back seat of Mrs Hewitt's

elderly Metro, with Karen sitting beside her mother in front of him, heading down to Portsmouth for a day by the sea looking round warships. He was looking forward to it enormously, though at one point it looked as if he wasn't going to get there.

Mrs Hewitt had suggested they have lunch when they got to the museum, but Bernard found, halfway there, that he was extremely hungry. And thirsty. He had a ten-pound note in his pocket that his father had given him as spending money, but he felt a little shy of asking Mrs Hewitt to stop so he could buy something to eat, when she had clearly made other plans.

And then he realized that he did not have to ask her at all. Looking out of the window he could see a garage coming up on the right and, as the car drove past, he pressed the button on his watch.

The world stopped. Bernard stepped out of the car, crossed through the frozen traffic to the garage on the other side of the road and walked into the shop on the forecourt. All he had to do was help himself to whatever he wanted and leave the money by the till.

In the shop, Bernard walked across to the fridge section containing the sandwiches. The door was a heavy one and he had to put the watch in his pocket so he could use both hands to pull it open. A pleasant tune played quietly on the garage music machine and he hummed along as he slowly debated what he might have.

'If there's anything you can't reach I could pass it down for you,' said a voice.

Bernard nearly jumped out of his skin. He spun round to see a middle-aged woman smiling helpfully down at him.

It was impossible. Nothing moved in frozen time. Nothing. That was the whole point.

'I'm sorry,' the woman stepped back apologetically. 'I didn't mean to startle you, I just thought if there was something you couldn't reach, I . . .' Her voice trailed off. 'You're quite right. Never talk to strangers. I'll just go and pay for my petrol.'

Bernard stared after her and his brain slowly registered several facts. The woman was walking over to the cashier who smiled and asked which pump she had been using. There was music playing. Outside, a car pulled into the forecourt . . .

He thrust a hand into his pocket and pulled out the watch. The hand marking the seconds ticked steadily round the face and, when he pressed the button at the top, the hand stopped. So did the music and the woman at the cash desk . . .

Bernard clicked the watch twice more to check, but he already knew what had happened. When he put the watch in his pocket to pull open the door of the drinks cabinet, he must have accidentally pressed the button to start time again. He ran outside but, as he feared, Mrs Hewitt's car was no longer where he had left it. When time had restarted, the car had carried on going. Bernard was not sure how long it had taken for him to realize what had happened and press the watch again, but it was long enough for the car to be completely out of sight. Shading his eyes and standing on the bonnet of a frozen BMW, he looked vainly down the road, but there was no sign of it.

It was a worrying situation, but not necessarily too serious. All he had to do, Bernard thought, was walk until he caught up with the car and get back in, hopefully before Karen or her mother realized he had gone.

But it was the walking that worried him. His legs were still aching slightly from playing in the football match and he would be on his feet most of the afternoon. If he had to walk a couple of miles down the road as well . . . It was probably this, in the end, that made him decide to borrow the bicycle.

There was a camper van on the road ahead, with two children's bicycles strapped to a frame at the back. Bernard took the keys from the camper van's ignition and found the one that unlocked the bikes. After taking one down, he wrote a note saying that he would leave it somewhere further up the road, and apologizing for any inconvenience this might cause. After a brief pause, while he sat on the garage forecourt to eat his sandwich and have a drink, he set off.

Riding the bicycle made the journey very simple. None of the other traffic was moving, so Bernard could weave in and out of the other cars and, although there was no gravity to help him freewheel down the hills, there was no gravity to make it difficult going up, either, and he made very good progress, until he came to a road junction.

It was a roundabout with a choice of five different exits and Bernard had no idea which one he should take. There was a police sergeant sitting in a patrol car at one of the exits so he rode over to ask him.

He got off the bicycle, took the watch from his pocket and, remembering Aunt Bee's warning about appearing suddenly in front of people, stood behind the policeman, before pressing the watch.

'Excuse me.' He leant forward so the policeman could see him. 'Could you tell me which is the road to Portsmouth?'

The policeman nodded with his head to point the direction.

'Third exit. Straight across the roundabout.'

'Thank you.' Bernard was about to turn away when the sergeant stopped him.

'Hoi!' he beckoned Bernard back. 'You're not planning to cycle there, are you?'

'Well . . . yes, I was.' Bernard hesitated. 'Shouldn't I?'

'Without a helmet? Do you know how dangerous that is? Have you any idea how fast the cars go along this road?'

Before Bernard could reply, there was a crackle from the car radio and a voice called, 'Nine five. Location, please.'

'You wait there.'

As the policeman turned to answer the radio, Bernard decided that waiting would not be a good idea. Pressing the button on his watch to freeze time, he got on his bike and pedalled off down the road.

About half a mile later, he found Mrs Hewitt's car pulling out to overtake a lorry. He left the bicycle on the grass verge with another note saying thank you to the people he had borrowed it from, and climbed in. Settling himself comfortably in the seat, he pressed the button on his watch.

'You're very quiet in the back there,' said Mrs Hewitt. 'Is everything all right?'

'Fine,' said Bernard. 'Absolutely fine.'

The trip to Portsmouth was a great success. As well as seeing HMS *Victory*, the children took a boat ride round the harbour and toured HMS *Warrior*, the first ironclad battleship in the world. They were all things that Bernard would have enjoyed at any time, but like everything else, they were even more exciting while he had the watch.

The watch meant that if you wanted a closer look at the cannon, you could go as close as you liked. If you wanted to try on Nelson's hat, or lie in a hammock, you could. And if you wanted to see what was the other side of the 'No Entry' signs, you could stop time and go and find out.

It was fun, too, to answer Mrs Hewitt's questions the same way he had answered questions in class the day before. When she asked the children if either of them knew which famous battle HMS *Victory* had fought in, he was able (after using the watch to consult a guidebook) not only to say that it was the battle of Trafalgar, but that it had been fought on 21 October 1805. Mrs Hewitt was visibly impressed.

And he enjoyed spending time with Karen as well. She did not say a great deal, in fact he afterwards remembered that she said almost nothing at all, but that might have been one of the reasons he liked being with her. She was a very peaceful person somehow. And he liked the way she smiled at the things he said. She had a nice smile.

Mrs Hewitt was delighted that the day had been such a success. The children had obviously enjoyed it, she had been enormously impressed by Bernard's knowledge of naval history, and it was not until they were getting ready to leave that she became concerned that the day had left him overtired.

It was Karen who pointed out how pale he had become, even before Bernard himself realized anything was wrong. Then, as they walked back to the car, he found his legs becoming wobbly, his vision becoming blurred, and a strange buzzing sensation filled his head.

He was quite relieved when Mrs Hewitt suggested he stretch out on the back seat and try to rest on the journey home. He lay down, closed his eyes and was asleep almost immediately.

Sergeant Palmer had been a policeman for nearly fourteen years and had seen a good many strange things in that time, but he knew it was not going to be easy to write a report about this one.

The two people at the police station claimed that a bicycle had been stolen from the back of their campervan while they were driving along the road.

They also said the thief had sellotaped a note to the steering wheel saying where he had taken the bicycle and why.

How anyone could take a bike from a van travelling at fifty miles an hour down a dual carriageway, and why they would want to leave a message once they had done it, defeated Sergeant Palmer completely. But he had found the bike on the grass verge on the road to Portsmouth with another note taped to the handlebars.

It read: *'Thank you again, and I am sorry if taking this caused any trouble, but it really was an emergency. Sorry. Thank you. Sorry again.'* It was written in the same round, clear hand as the first, and Sergeant Palmer was at a loss to explain it.

He had recognized the bicycle when they found it. It was the one the boy who asked the way to Portsmouth had been riding. The boy who had suddenly disappeared while he was answering the car radio. Sergeant Palmer promised himself that, if he saw the lad again, he would get him to answer a few questions.

He had no doubt that, if he *did* see the boy again, he would recognize him. Like all good policemen, he had an excellent memory for faces.

It was not until they got home that Mrs Hewitt realized anything was wrong. She thought Bernard had been asleep during the journey and it was only when she tried to wake him, to tell him they were home, that she realized he was not sleeping at all, but deeply unconscious.

In some alarm, she told Karen to get Mr Beasley and then ran indoors herself to ring for an ambulance.

Chapter Five
VISITING TIME

Mr Beasley was an energetic man – running your own business is something that requires a good deal of energy – but he did not feel very energetic as he walked up the steps to Aunt Bee's house. He had had no sleep the night before, he had not eaten properly, and he was very tired.

He pushed open the front door and was about to walk through into the drawing room when Mrs Donaldson, the cleaning lady, called from the top of the stairs to tell him that Mrs Temperley was in the conservatory.

Mr Beasley thanked her and set off down the hall. He knew this house almost as well as his own. His wife had lived here before they were married. The wedding reception and Bernard's christening party had been held here and, when his wife died three years after Bernard was born, this was where everyone had gathered, to stand in their stiff suits and dark clothes after the funeral.

He had seen much less of the place recently, despite living just down the road. The business absorbed most of his energies. Bernard spent a lot of time here, of course, after school and in the daytime during the holidays, while Mr Beasley was at work.

'You'll never believe what I've got here.'

In the warmth of the conservatory, Aunt Bee was holding up a jam jar, a hand cupped over the top to prevent the insect inside from escaping.

'It's a Dewick's Plusia!'

Mr Beasley tried to sound appreciative as he examined what seemed to be a very ordinary brown moth. He had never understood why Aunt Bee was so interested in them, though she had always been a woman of enthusiasms. He remembered how worried everyone had been when she started making her own fireworks.

'He's not supposed to be in this country at all,' the old lady continued. 'This time of year he should be somewhere in the Mediterranean. Must have got his wires crossed and flown north instead of south.'

She held the moth up to the light for a better look.

'They only live about six weeks, you know. And it looks like this one's spent most of his life flying in the wrong direction.' She put down the jam jar upside down on the table and took off her glasses.

'Well, John. What can I do for you?'

'Bernard asked me to give you this.' Mr Beasley reached into his pocket and took out the watch, wrapped in a handkerchief. 'He said to thank you very much for lending it to him and he's sorry he didn't get it back to you when he said he would, but he's been ill.'

'Ill?' Aunt Bee looked up sharply. 'Why? What's happened to him?'

'We're not sure.' Mr Beasley ran his fingers through his hair and stifled a yawn. 'The woman next door took him to Portsmouth yesterday, to the Naval Heritage Museum, and when they got home he was unconscious in the back of the car.'

'Oh goodness!' Aunt Bee's concern showed openly on her face. 'Where is he?'

'In hospital. They say it's not serious. Some form of anaemia, but they don't know what caused it so they're keeping him in till they find out.'

'Oh! I should have known!'

Aunt Bee banged a fist on the arm of her chair in exasperation.

'I don't think there's any way you could have known, really,' said Mr Beasley. 'One minute he was fine and the next he was out like a light. Nothing any of us could have done.' He paused. 'Well, I just came to give you the watch. It was the first thing Bernard spoke about when he came round. He was worried you might think he'd walked off with it.'

'That was very thoughtful of him.' Aunt Bee put the watch in her pocket and carefully folded the handkerchief before passing it back. 'I shall call in and thank him myself, tomorrow. He'll be allowed visitors by then, I presume?'

'Oh yes. He'll be delighted to see you.' Mr Beasley yawned again, and stood up. 'Well, I just wanted you to know. If you don't mind, I'd better get home.'

'Won't you stay for lunch?' Aunt Bee stood up as well. 'You look as if you could do with something to eat.'

Mr Beasley said that, though he would like to stay, there wasn't time. He had been at the hospital most of the last eighteen hours and he still had to fill in the government form about how many hours a week his drivers had been on the road. There was a lot of work to catch up on.

When he got home, however, and sat at his desk with the papers spread out before him, he fell asleep almost immediately, his head slumped on his chest. And while he slept, he dreamt uneasily of a giant moth with a face like a juggernaut lorry, flying determinedly to Iceland, when he knew it was supposed to be going to Istanbul.

Bernard rather enjoyed being in hospital. A children's ward is a very pleasant place to be as long as you are not feeling ill and, since he had woken up, Bernard had never felt better.

He had his own television at the bottom of the bed, with a computer games-machine plugged into it and dozens of games. There was no schoolwork, he could choose what he wanted to eat and, down the corridor, there was an entire room full of books and toys to play with whenever he liked. The doctors said they wanted to keep him in hospital until they found out why he had become ill and, as far as Bernard was concerned, they could keep him as long as they liked.

On Monday, he had five visitors and all of them brought presents. His father called in at lunchtime with a personal stereo and half a dozen CDs that the girl in the shop had told him were the sort of thing a boy Bernard's age would like. At four o'clock, Karen and her mother arrived and Karen gave him a pile of comics while Mrs Hewitt produced a book of mathematical puzzles that she said were good for keeping the mind active even when you had to stay in bed.

No sooner had the two of them left, than Miss Picot appeared with a 'Get Well' card signed by everyone in his class, and a box of chocolates. She said how sorry she was that Bernard was ill, but that she hoped he would be better soon as they really needed him for the match the following Saturday. It was the start of the Schools' League and there was no one else she could trust to play in goal.

Perhaps the visitor Bernard appreciated most, however, was Aunt Bee, who arrived in the evening, just as visiting time was coming to an end, striding across the ward with her stick. She put a bag of grapes on Bernard's lap and looked at him carefully before asking how he felt.

'I'm fine,' said Bernard. 'They're only keeping me here so they can find out what caused the anaemia.'

'Yes,' Aunt Bee hesitated. 'Well . . . I have an apology to make there. You see, it was me.'

'You?' Bernard frowned. 'Are you sure?'

Aunt Bee nodded. 'Not directly, of course, but it's the watch that does it. It uses up the iron molecules in your body. Philip and I often wondered why, but we never found out. He passed out half a dozen times before we realized what was happening. You're all right as long as you drink a suitable iron tonic though.' She produced a large brown bottle from her bag and put it on the table by Bernard's bed. 'Which is why I put some of this in your drink each day.'

Bernard remembered the odd taste of the lemonade his Aunt had given him.

'But it occurred to me,' the old lady continued, 'that you might have used the watch to pour the drink away without my knowing, because you didn't like the taste or something.'

This was exactly what Bernard had done. In frozen time he had not been able to pour anything, of course, but he had taken his glass out to the kitchen, turned it upside down over the sink, lifted it up and returned to the sitting room leaving the liquid behind.

'I'm sorry,' he said. 'I didn't know.'

'Not your fault.' Aunt Bee reached into a pocket. 'And there's no real harm done. I checked on your notes in the nurse's office before I came in. As long as you remember to take a tablespoon of that every day –' she pointed to the bottle by his bed – 'you shouldn't have any more problems.'

She reached into her pocket, took out the watch, and put it on the bed beside Bernard.

'But if you're going to have this on a permanent

basis, you'll have to promise to remember to take some every day.'

Bernard picked up the watch. 'Permanent?'

'I can't give it to you,' said Aunt Bee. 'Not yet. But I want you to look after it for me. For a month or two. Would you do that?'

'I can keep it? For a month?' Bernard could hardly believe his ears.

'I'll still be seeing you every day, of course. After school.' Aunt Bee was burrowing in her bag again. 'So you can tell me how you're getting on. And I'll remind you then about taking the tonic. Here, you'd better have this while we're at it.'

From her bag, she produced the watch chain. At one end of it was a clip, which she joined to the ring at the top of the watch and, at the other, were two gold rods, hinged in the middle like a pair of scissors.

'You hold these straight to start with.' Aunt Bee reached across and threaded the rods at the end of the chain through a buttonhole in Bernard's pyjamas. 'Then you open them out . . .' She opened the rods till they were at ninety degrees to each other. 'So that it can't come out again. Helps you not to lose it, you see?'

Bernard was barely listening. He was sitting there, gazing at the watch in his hand.

'Thanks, Auntie,' he said, eventually.

'A hospital's quite a good place to have the watch.' Aunt Bee sat back in her chair. 'Lots of interesting things going on. On my way in, I passed an operating theatre where they're doing a kidney transplant. Rather fun. You might want to take a look. Oh, and one more thing . . .' She pointed to a small indentation in the side of the watch. 'If you want to look at the insides, you push there with your thumbnail. Not that you'll be any the wiser when you do, of course. Didn't help me or Philip, but you ought to know about it.'

Aunt Bee reached across to take the watch and was about to show him what she meant, when a nurse came in and said it was time for visitors to leave.

Aunt Bee did not protest. She said it was probably just as well, as she had already kept the taxi waiting longer than she had promised. She picked up her stick, bent down so that Bernard could give her a kiss, told him she would be back tomorrow, and left.

When Mr Beasley got home from work that evening, he found a note under a milk bottle on the front step asking him to call next door.

He rang the bell and Mrs Hewitt let him in.

'I've got the pyjamas for you,' she explained, as she ushered Mr Beasley into her sitting room. 'Two pairs. And I got him a toothbrush as well. I hope you don't mind, only I noticed the one he had was a bit worn.'

'Not at all,' said Mr Beasley. 'I'm very grateful.'

As he took out his wallet, he looked round and saw that the front room of the flat, a combined kitchen and dining room, was as neat as Mrs Hewitt herself. There was a pile of neatly folded ironing on a chair by the door. The table was neatly laid for supper and even the saucepans on the cooker had their handles neatly pointing in the same direction.

As Mrs Hewitt produced a neatly written bill setting out how much the pyjamas and toothbrush had cost, he could hear Karen practising her cello in another room.

'You've been very kind,' he said. 'I should have realized he'd grown out of the others, but . . . well, you know how it is.'

On Saturday evening, when they had all gone to the hospital and after it was clear Bernard was going to be all right, the ward sister had suggested Mr Beasley go home and pick up the things his son would need, like his sponge bag and pyjamas.

Mr Beasley had not been able to find any pyjamas, however, and eventually remembered that these days Bernard usually slept in his vest. Mrs Hewitt had offered to buy some new ones for him on her way back from work on Monday.

'And I never thanked you properly for taking him out on Saturday,' Mr Beasley said, as he handed over the money. 'He really enjoyed himself. He was telling me all about it at lunchtime today.'

'It was a pleasure to have him. He's a very clever boy.' Mrs Hewitt smiled. 'Next time I'll try and bring him back while he's still conscious.'

As she showed Mr Beasley to the door, she did not add that she had been tempted to buy a new pair of pyjamas for him as well. She had noticed the ones he had been wearing under his sweater when he answered the door on Saturday had had holes in both knees. How a man could run a highly successful business employing dozens of people and not make sure he had a decent pair of pyjamas puzzled her. Though she had to admit he had looked quite respectable today. In fact, in his suit and tie and with his face shaved he had looked more than respectable. Almost good-looking.

Back in his own house, Mr Beasley scooped the dishes from the table into the sink, peeled back the foil cover from the prawn curry he had bought on the way home and put it in the microwave. As he waited for the food to reheat, he found himself thinking a little enviously of the food Mrs Hewitt had been preparing next door. A proper meal, sitting at a table, with clean plates and cutlery . . .

But it was only a passing thought. While he waited for his supper to heat up, he started dialling a number on his mobile phone. He had a lorry stuck outside Milan that needed a new distributor cap and somehow, before the evening was out, he had to find a garage that was still awake and prepared to do something about it.

When his aunt had left, Bernard pressed with his thumbnail at the place she had indicated and the back of the watch flipped open. Inside, there were no cogs and springs, no escapement or ratchets, only a solid block of something white, which, he realized as he looked closer, was not really solid at all. It moved. It was a white light that coiled and swirled and had a depth that, as you looked at it, seemed to stretch into for ever.

He reached out with a finger to touch it, and then wondered if it was safe. In the end, curiosity overcame the fear and he pushed his forefinger gently into the light. Apart from a slight coldness, he felt nothing at all, though the sight of his finger disappearing into the watch was a little alarming. It was simply absorbed, though it looked perfectly normal as he pulled it back. Bernard had the feeling that the whiteness inside the watch was probably as capable of absorbing his hand or even his whole arm.

'Goodness, what have you got there?' asked the nurse who had come back to turn Bernard's light out. Hastily, he closed the watch before answering.

'It's a watch I was given,' he said. 'By a friend.'

The nurse smiled. 'Quite a special friend, I'd say, to give you something like that.'

'Yes,' said Bernard. 'Yes, she is.'

The nurse drew the curtains and was about to turn the light out when Bernard asked if she could leave it on a bit longer so that he could read.

'I'm afraid not.' The nurse was very firm. 'Not tonight. There's no time.' Her finger reached out for the light switch but, before she touched it, Bernard pressed the button on his watch.

The nurse froze, and Bernard took up one of the comics Karen had brought. He might take a tour of the hospital later, he thought, but for the moment he would lie there and read. He held the comic in the air above his head and, in frozen time, it hung in exactly the right place above his eyes.

He settled down on his pillow and smiled as he remembered what the nurse had said. 'No time!' She could not have been more wrong.

Chapter Six

SAVING TIME

In the weeks that followed, those around him could not help but notice how Bernard had changed. His teachers all noticed the extraordinary improvement in his class work. Mr Tree remarked on several occasions how calm and unworried he always seemed these days, and even Mr Beasley, busy as he was negotiating a new contract to import tomatoes from Greece, noticed how his son had always done whatever you asked him to do, almost before you finished speaking.

And, of course, *everyone* noticed the football.

Bernard had rapidly risen from being the newest member of the school football team to its undisputed star. Since he joined, they had not lost a single match and, to Miss Picot's delight, they were already into the last sixteen in the Schools' League. The reason was very simple. When Bernard played in goal, the other side never scored.

Ever.

Miss Picot said it was the most extraordinary thing she had ever seen and that Bernard's ability to know where the ball was going to be and put himself in a position to stop it, was little short of miraculous. Younger children would stop him and ask for his autograph in the school corridors. Louis Hugh-Jones, would make a point of consulting with him before a game, and Mr Tree would ask anxiously after his health on the day of a match. Bernard rather enjoyed it all.

'If someone gave you three wishes,' he told his aunt, one day after school, 'a watch like this should be the first thing you should wish for. And you should probably use the other two wishes to get a couple of spares. It's the answer to everything, really, isn't it?'

'You think so?' Aunt Bee was pouring some iron tonic on to a spoon.

'Definitely,' said Bernard. 'I mean, you can do anything with the watch, can't you? If anything's wrong, you can change it. If you don't like being where you are, you can go somewhere else. If you want to do something, you can just do it . . . You can do anything!'

'Not quite anything,' Aunt Bee said quietly as she held out the spoon, 'but I'm glad you're enjoying it.'

The one person who did not appear to notice any change in Bernard, or who did not say anything about it if she did, was Karen. But this may have been because she had not known Bernard very well before he had the watch.

The two children had seen a good deal of each other since the trip to Portsmouth and Bernard's time in hospital. Mrs Hewitt took them out every Saturday now (though she was careful to make sure Bernard did not get overtired) and occasionally took them to the cinema on a Sunday as well.

For Bernard, with a father too busy to take him anywhere and an aunt who couldn't walk without a stick, these trips out were yet another part of how wonderful life had become since he had been given the watch. So far, they had visited the Bristol Exploratory, the theme park at Alton Towers, the Beaulieu Motor Museum and Marwell Zoological Gardens.

Of the four, Marwell had been Bernard's favourite. It was an interesting enough place in itself, but with a watch it was even better. It is one thing to stand in a viewing gallery and watch a crocodile yawn, but it is something else again to climb into the enclosure and put your hand on its back and peer down its jaws. To stand right next to a lion, to stroke the fur on an ocelot, or to walk under a giraffe had given Bernard a delight he could still remember.

And it was at Marwell, too, that Karen started to talk. Walking round the enclosures while Mrs Hewitt sat in the café, she suddenly started telling Bernard how she had always wanted a dog, but that the flat they lived in was too small. Then she told him how she had once been given a rat called Boris by her father, but how she had to keep it away from her mother who was allergic to them. And how she had come back from school one day to find Boris had escaped and had never been found, though she had searched for days.

It was the first time Bernard had heard Karen say anything about herself or, indeed, say anything much at all, and it was that day that he realized they had, for some reason, become friends.

It was a friendship that Mrs Hewitt was openly relieved to see and which seemed to have several advantages for her daughter. Bernard was clearly an exceptionally clever boy and she noticed how this had encouraged Karen to do even better in her own work in class. The children usually walked to school together, as well, which was a useful guarantee that there would be no repeat of the bullying incident that had unsettled Karen so badly at the start of term. And there was also the matter of the money. Mr Beasley, as soon as Mrs Hewitt had started making Saturday trips a regular event, had insisted that he contribute to expenses and the money he gave her for petrol and tickets was, in fact, what enabled the trips to happen at all.

But the advantages went both ways and how useful it was for Bernard to have a friend like Karen, he found out a few days before half-term.

Aunt Bee had impressed on Bernard from the start that, if possible, he was never to leave the watch anywhere someone else might find it or pick it up. He must never leave it in his coat, for instance, or out on his desk, or put it down somewhere while he was getting changed. The watch must always be either in his pocket or in his hand. All the time.

There was one place, however, where it was difficult for him to do this. Once a fortnight, on a Wednesday afternoon, the class went swimming in the local baths and, short of taking the watch into the water with him, Bernard had no choice but to leave it somewhere else.

Usually, he left it with his aunt, but on this particular Wednesday, when he slipped out of the playground at lunchtime and went round to her house, she was not there. Mrs Donaldson said she had had to go to the doctor's, but would be back at about three. She asked if there was anything she could do to help, but Bernard said no thank you, and returned to school.

He thought carefully before deciding what he should do instead. There were three people in his class who would not be going swimming. They were the people who played in the school orchestra and needed to practice for a concert the following Saturday. One of the three was Karen, and Bernard decided to put the watch in his school bag, carefully wrapped in a football shirt, and leave the bag with her.

Karen was already in the hall, tuning up her cello, when he asked her if this would be all right.

'OK,' she said.

'It'll only be while you're practising,' Bernard explained. 'And I'll be back at quarter-past three.'

'OK,' said Karen.

'The thing is . . .' Bernard hesitated. 'The thing is, it's got my watch in. And it's quite valuable. So if you could make sure nothing happens to it?'

'OK,' said Karen, and she took the bag and put it under her chair.

And everything would have been all right if the coach taking Bernard's class back to school from the swimming baths had not broken down in the High Street on the way. Karen stood at the school gates for fifteen minutes before deciding she could not wait any longer. Her mother would not only be worrying that something had happened to her, but waiting for the milk she had asked Karen to get from the corner shop on her way home. It was outside the shop, when she got there, that she met the Ryan twins.

On her first day at school, at the start of term, Karen had been involved in a playground fight with the Ryan twins, which had badly frightened her and got the twins into a good deal of trouble. For reasons she had never understood they had taken a dislike to her, and they had made it clear on several occasions since that they had not changed their minds.

They were big girls and not very nice, and when they stepped out to block Karen's path, she did not know what to do. Later, she realized there were a good many things she could have done. She could have run into the shop or screamed for help at the top of her voice or simply turned round and run away, but for some reason she did none of them. She just stood there, staring at the pavement, clutching Bernard's bag to her chest, saying nothing.

She had no idea why the twins disliked her so much or why they were picking on her, but when one of them tried to grab Bernard's bag from her arms, her grip on it tightened and she refused to let go.

It was an ugly incident, though fortunately it did not last very long. When Mr Singh came out of his shop, the twins ran off. He came over to see if Karen, who was lying on the ground, was all right and found she was bleeding from a cut lip, had a bad scratch on one arm and several bruises down her legs.

But in her arms, very tightly, she was still holding the bag. And when he brought her into the shop to sit down and recover, she was still holding it, and refused to put it down.

Even when her mother arrived to take her home, she still would not let go of the bag.

Bernard had already heard most of what had happened before he called at Karen's flat. Mrs Hewitt let him in before going back to dabbing at the bruises on Karen's legs with witch hazel and some cotton wool.

'Are you OK?' asked Bernard.

'No, she certainly is not,' said Mrs Hewitt. 'She was set upon outside the shop. Two children tried to steal your bag from her, but she wouldn't let them have it.'

'Yes, I heard.' Bernard looked across at Karen.

'Thank you.' He looked again at the bruises on her legs and the scratch on her arm.

'Do you know who it was?'

'She'd never seen them before,' said Mrs Hewitt. 'She's not even sure what they looked like. But we're going to report the whole thing to the police as soon as I've finished this. Here . . .' She gave her daughter the cotton wool. 'Hold this on the bruise. I'm going to get an ice pack.'

When Mrs Hewitt had gone, Bernard asked Karen what had happened, but she did not answer.

He thought about it. There were a limited number of options really.

'The Ryan twins? Is that who it was?'

Karen nodded.

'Aren't you going to tell anyone?'

Karen shrugged. 'It'll only make them do something worse the next time, won't it?'

'No,' said Bernard. 'I think it'll be worse if you *don't* tell someone. But it's all right. You don't have to worry.'

'Don't I?' Karen looked miserably up at Bernard. 'Why? What are you going to do?'

'I'm not sure yet,' said Bernard.

There was a stony expression on his normally open, friendly face. He stood up and slung his bag over his shoulder.

'But you don't have to bother about them doing something worse next time. There isn't going to be a next time.'

★

'And what did you do,' asked Aunt Bee, 'to make sure there wouldn't be a next time?'

She had been asleep when Bernard came round, lying on one of the sofas in the drawing room with some pillows under her head and a blanket over her legs. Bernard was just leaving so as not to disturb her, when she opened her eyes.

Over a glass of milk and some biscuits, he told her what had happened to Karen and the bag and the watch.

'So what did you do?' Aunt Bee repeated.

What Bernard had done, after leaving Karen's flat, was press the button on his watch and go in search of the Ryan twins. He had found them, in the gathering twilight, sitting on the swings in the park, laughing.

The temptation to do something horrid to them there and then was very great. He wanted to drag them off the swings and kick them the way they had kicked Karen, but in the end he didn't. What he did was take them to the police. In frozen time, he started by pulling Laura off the swing so that she was sitting in mid-air, and then pushed her across the park until he came to the railings. He straightened her body out, lifted it upwards and hung her from the top of the railings by the hood on the back of her coat. Then he went back and did the same thing to her sister.

He wrote a short account of what the twins had done on a piece of paper, put it in the hands of a policeman walking down the opposite side of the road, and then wrote two more notes, which he put in the twin's pockets. These said that if they ever laid a finger on Karen again, he promised they would face something much worse than being hung up on some railings.

'Well, you seem to have dealt with it all very decisively.' Aunt Bee lay back on her pillows. 'I'm sure the policeman will sort everything out.'

'I hope so.' Bernard nodded rather absent-mindedly. 'And I think what I did will have frightened the twins a bit.'

'Yes,' his Aunt nodded. 'I'd say you'll have frightened them quite a lot.'

'And I'll keep an eye on Karen,' said Bernard. 'Walk home with her from school, that sort of thing.'

'Yes, that might be a good idea,' said Aunt Bee.

Bernard looked thoughtfully for several seconds at the watch in his hand.

'What is it? What's the matter?'

'I didn't realize,' said Bernard.

'Realize what?'

'I thought it was just fun.' Bernard was still looking at his watch. 'I thought it just helped you do things when you didn't have enough time, but it does a lot more than that, doesn't it?'

His aunt did not answer, but she was looking carefully at Bernard through half-closed eyes.

'I mean, I could have done anything to those girls, couldn't I? I could have hurt them, I could have . . . I could have killed them if I'd wanted. No one would have known.'

'Well, I'm glad you didn't,' said Aunt Bee. 'Kill them, I mean. That's not really what the watch is for, is it?'

Bernard helped himself to a biscuit from the plate on the table and, as he ate it, remembered that his aunt had used a very similar phrase the first day she had given him the watch. She had said then that what the watch was for was the only question worth asking. He wondered what she had meant.

'I've been meaning to ask,' he said. 'What *is* the watch for exactly?'

But Aunt Bee did not reply. Her head on her chest, breathing deeply, she had fallen asleep again and Bernard, after waiting a few moments, gently pulled up the blanket to make sure she stayed warm.

Twenty minutes later, when his father's car appeared outside, Bernard gathered up his things and left, as quietly as he could, so as not to disturb her.

Sergeant Palmer got home a little later than usual that evening and, as he laid the table while his wife cooked the tea, he told her why.

The first surprise had been the note that appeared in his hand as he was walking down Romans Road towards the park. Who had put it there and how was a complete mystery, while its contents were, if anything, even stranger.

The note read: '*There are two girls hanging on the railings who attacked Karen Hewitt outside Mr Singh's shop after school today. Please could you make sure they do not do this again. Thank you.'*

To Sergeant Palmer's surprise there were indeed two girls hanging on the railings the other side of the road and they were none other than the Ryan twins, whom the sergeant had dealt with on several previous occasions. They would not say who had put them there. The girls, looking thoroughly frightened, insisted that they had no idea how they got there.

Then there had been the phone call from the Headmaster of the local Junior School, wanting to talk about one of his pupils being attacked outside the local shop and at least part of the truth had finally emerged. Sergeant Palmer had spent the rest of the afternoon talking to the girls and their parents, trying to work out what should be done with them.

But, at the end of it all, he was still left with the most puzzling part of the business. Sergeant Palmer had recognized the writing on the note that so mysteriously appeared in his hand straightaway. It was exactly the same handwriting as the note the people in the campervan said they had found on their steering wheel.

He did not tell anyone about it, apart from his wife. Notes that appear out of nowhere are one of those things, like seeing a flying saucer, that are best not reported when you are hoping for promotion to Inspector. But he kept it, as he had the others, determined that one day he would solve the mystery.

Sergeant Palmer was a good policeman and, like all good policemen, he knew how to wait.

Chapter Seven
TIME SHARE

Bernard would probably have given Karen a birthday present anyway but, after the way she had hung on to his bag when the Ryan twins tried to take it away, he wanted to get her something special. And he realized, as soon as he started thinking about it, that the present he wanted to give her was a rat.

When she had told him at Marwell about Boris, the rat she had lost, she had also told him she still had its cage. She was hoping one day to be able to buy a replacement, though a trip to the pet shop made it clear that rats, even small ones, cost more than she could afford at the moment.

Bernard, however, was not worried about how expensive rats were as he had no intentions of buying one. He did not need to. He could catch one.

From the first day Aunt Bee had given him the watch and he had touched the wings of the sparrow flying across the playground, Bernard had found that, in frozen time, he could catch almost anything. A fly buzzing around his bedroom or a moth loose in Aunt Bee's conservatory was no problem for Bernard. He could simply freeze time, scoop it up in his hands and do with it what he liked.

The same principle applied to all sorts of wildlife. Animals that would normally have hidden at the slightest warning of an approaching human were still out in the open when Bernard came by in frozen time. In his own garden he had seen hedgehogs, moles, squirrels and even a fox. He had not come across any rats so far but, as it happened, he had recently been told exactly where to look, if he wanted to find one.

Mr Wickerstaffe, the school caretaker, had told Mr Tree that insecure lids on the waste food bins, combined with the building work the other side of the fence, had encouraged the existence of a small colony of rats somewhere behind the school kitchens. The headmaster warned the children to stay away from the area as poison would be laid down over half-term, and it was then that Bernard had realized he had the perfect opportunity to get his friend exactly the birthday present she most wanted.

Karen's birthday was on the Saturday and, early that morning, Bernard set off for the school armed with his watch and a biscuit tin, in the lid of which he had already made some holes so that the rat, when he caught it, would be able to breathe.

It was even easier than he expected. In frozen time, he climbed over the gate into the school playground and walked round to the back of the main building where the kitchens and dustbins were. The area seemed very clean and tidy but, on the other side of the fence, where the new extension was being built to the fire station, there were large piles of rubbish that looked very promising. Using a stick to lift up some of the pieces of cardboard and wood, Bernard found a rat almost immediately.

In fact, he found five. Frozen, motionless, round the remains of a discarded curry, they were not quite the same as the rats in the pet shop. Instead of delicate-looking creatures with white coats and slender pink paws, these were large, powerful-looking animals with matted, dark-brown fur and pointed yellow teeth.

Bernard chose the rat that had the fewest scars, picked it up by the tail and put it in the biscuit tin. He returned to his house to pick up Karen's birthday card and took it, with the tin under his arm, next door to Karen.

'That's very kind of you, Bernard!' said Mrs Hewitt when she answered the door and Bernard told her why he was there. 'You've just got time to see her before she goes.'

As well as being Karen's birthday, Saturday was the day Mr Tree was taking the school orchestra to Southampton to play in the concert for which they had been practising all term. Karen had been particularly looking forward to it as it meant they were all going to be on television.

'Perhaps you could give her a hand bringing out

the cello,' said Mrs Hewitt. 'Only Mr Tree could be here any minute and we don't want to keep him waiting.

Bernard walked down the corridor to Karen's bedroom and pressed the button on his watch before going inside. He thought it would be nicer to give Karen the rat in its cage rather than the biscuit tin so, in frozen time, he let himself into her room and collected the cage from the bottom of the wardrobe where he knew it was kept.

As he transferred the rat from the tin, he saw there was blood coming from its nose – the result of its frantic efforts to escape. He got a tissue from the box by the bed to wipe the worst of it away and it was as he did so that he noticed Karen.

She was sitting on the bed, with her hands in her lap, looking at the ground and there was a tear frozen halfway down one cheek.

Gathering up his biscuit tin and the rat cage, Bernard wondered what had happened to upset his friend on her birthday. As he went back out to the hall with the cage, he also wondered why she was sitting on the bed in her vest, if Mr Tree was due to arrive at any moment. She was supposed to be leaving in a few minutes, but she was not even dressed and her cello was still out of its case, leaning in the corner of the room by the music stand.

Leaving the tin on the floor and holding the cage, he knocked on the door and went inside.

'Happy birthday!' Bernard held up his gift. 'It's for you.'

'Oh.' Karen looked up briefly and wiped away the tear. 'Hello, Bernard.'

It was not quite the response he had hoped for.

'It's a rat,' he explained, bringing it closer. 'To replace Boris.'

Karen looked at it.

'It's a wild one.'

'Yes.'

'You can't keep wild rats,' she said. 'If they bite you, you get Weil's disease and go blind.'

'Oh.'

Bernard put the cage on the floor and came and sat next to Karen on the bed.

'Is everything all right?'

For answer, Karen pointed to some clothes hanging on the back of the door.

'I'm supposed to be wearing those at the concert,' she said.

The clothes on the back of the door looked to Bernard like a man's tweed suit.

'I thought Mr Tree said you had to wear a black skirt and a white blouse.'

'He did. They gave me the wrong clothes at the cleaners. But I didn't realize till I took them out of the bag just now to get changed.'

'Oh,' said Bernard.

'There's going to be television cameras there,' said Karen, 'and when they show it, everyone's going to be wearing black and white, except me.'

'Can't you go back and get the right clothes?' asked Bernard.

'You mean go down, tell Mum, walk into town, go to the dry cleaners, change the clothes, walk back here, and get dressed?'

'Yes.'

'There isn't time, is there!'

Before Bernard could answer, there was the toot of a horn from outside and Mrs Hewitt's voice called from the front of the house.

'Karen? Karen, the minibus is here!'

Bernard was never quite sure why he did what he did next and, in a way, it was not something he decided to do at all. He just did it.

'Here. Take this.' He took the watch from his pocket and put it in Karen's hand. 'If you press the button on the top . . .' He pointed to the button at the top of the watch. 'Look, I'll explain later. Just do it.'

Karen looked at the watch, then at Bernard, then back at the watch.

From the hall, her mother called again. 'Karen, are you there?'

'Look, I know it sounds odd,' said Bernard, 'but try it. You'll know what I mean as soon as you do. Please, try it.'

Slowly, Karen reached up to press the button at the top of the watch.

And disappeared.

'You gave her the watch?' asked Aunt Bee.

Bernard nodded. 'I hope you don't mind.'

'Is she going to give it back?'

'Oh yes. She already did.' Bernard held up the watch to show he still had it. 'Straight away. Well, nearly.'

It had been an odd experience and now that Karen was safely on her way to Southampton with Mr Tree, he had come round to his aunt's to tell her what had happened.

Aunt Bee was in bed and the doctor had said she was to stay there for at least two weeks. The bed had been brought down to the drawing room and Mrs Donaldson was coming in each day in the evenings as well as at lunchtime, to make sure she had something to eat. Bernard's aunt lay there, propped up by a vast number of pillows.

'So what happened after your friend disappeared?' she asked.

What had happened was that Bernard had stared for a moment in panic at the place on the bed where Karen had been sitting and then spun round to find she was standing on the other side of the room.

Only now she was dressed in a smart black skirt and a clean white blouse, with her hair carefully brushed and with her cello packed in its case on the floor beside her. She was holding the watch in her hand and staring at it in astonishment.

'I knew there was something,' she said. 'I mean, I knew you'd got something that . . . but I never thought . . . I mean . . . Where did you get it?'

Bernard was about to reply when Mrs Hewitt's voice called impatiently again.

'Karen? Did you hear? The minibus is here!'

Bernard was slowly coming to grips with what had happened. 'You've been into town? To the cleaners?'

'Went into town, got my clothes, got these –' Karen pointed to some new earrings she was wearing – 'Came back, got changed, did my hair . . .' She looked at the watch in her hand again before passing it to Bernard. 'Did you find it, or did someone give it to you?'

Bernard could hear Mrs Hewitt opening the front door and calling to Mr Tree that Karen was on her way. 'You'll have to hear about it when you get back.' He picked up the cello. 'Come on. I'll give you a hand.'

'But you will tell me, won't you?' Karen gathered up her music. 'You promise?'

'I promise,' said Bernard.

Outside, Mr Tree and Mrs Hewitt were waiting by the minibus. As the Headmaster took the cello and started strapping it to the roof rack, Karen turned and gave Bernard a hug.

'Thanks for the birthday present, Bernard,' she said. 'I'll see you when I get back.'

She pulled open the door to get into the minibus.

'I'd forgotten it was your birthday,' said Mr Tree. 'What did Bernard give you?'

Karen barely hesitated. 'He gave me his time,' she said.

'A very good present.' Mr Tree smiled at Bernard. 'Good luck in the match this afternoon. I'm sorry I shan't be there, but I've told Miss Picot to ring me on the mobile straight after the final whistle.'

He climbed into the front and Bernard and Mrs Hewitt waved goodbye from the pavement as the van drove off.

'You've got a football match this afternoon?' asked Aunt Bee.

'It's the quarter finals,' said Bernard, 'of the Schools' League.' He looked at his aunt. 'I know you told me not to tell anyone, but it's all right, isn't it? That I let Karen borrow the watch?'

'I'm not sure.' Aunt Bee thought for a moment. 'It depends. It's exactly how I got the watch, of course –' she pointed to the photo on the table by her bed – 'when Philip decided to share it with me. But you need to be careful. Did you say your friend took some earrings from a shop while she was there?'

'Bought them,' Bernard corrected her. 'She had some birthday money and left it by the till with a note.'

'I see.' Aunt Bee nodded slowly. 'And if she wants to borrow the watch again, will you let her?'

Bernard said he thought that yes, he probably would, if Aunt Bee did not mind.

'And what if she borrows the watch and doesn't give it back?'

'I don't think she'd do that. She's . . .' Bernard looked for the right word. 'Well, she's nice.'

'It's a good start. But something as powerful as the watch can make even the nicest people behave strangely.' Aunt Bee lent back on her pillows before adding, 'If she is going to use the watch again, she'll need some iron tonic, won't she?'

'Yes.' Bernard had already thought of that. 'I'm going to put some in her drink.'

'Good idea. You haven't said anything to her about needing it yet?'

'Not yet.' Bernard hesitated a moment. 'To start with, I thought I'd just put it in her drink.'

'Very sensible,' said Aunt Bee. 'Very sensible.'

She had always thought Bernard was smarter than people gave him credit for. He might need more time than most for his schoolwork, but he picked up on the things that mattered very quickly indeed.

'Which only leaves us the question of what to do with him.'

Aunt Bee pointed to the biscuit tin on the floor from which odd thumps could be heard as the rat inside tried desperately to escape.

'Have you decided what you're going to do?'

What Bernard should do with the rat was something of a problem. Aunt Bee had confirmed that wild rats did not make ideal pets and could spread an alarming number of diseases. She had suggested that Bernard put it back where he had found it, but that would almost certainly mean it would be poisoned by Mr Wickerstaffe and he thought he owed it something after the discomfort he had caused it by keeping it in the tin.

Which was why, in the end, he took it round to the police station.

★

At the station, Sergeant Palmer was trying his best to sound patient and sympathetic.

'I'm not angry,' he repeated. 'I just want to know what happened.'

'But I told you!' The young constable was only three weeks out of training and blushing to the roots of his hair. 'I was standing at the desk and it just appeared there.'

'Appeared?' Sergeant Palmer lifted an eyebrow. 'You didn't close your eyes for a few minutes? A little doze perhaps? Nod off for a few seconds?'

'No.' Red-faced and embarrassed as he was, the constable stuck to his guns. 'I was wide awake. The desk was empty. Then suddenly there was the tin. I'm telling you, it appeared out of nowhere.'

Sergeant Palmer sighed. It was not biscuit tins appearing out of nowhere that bothered him about this business. Nor the fact that Constable Diderot had lifted the lid on this one and released a large and extremely vicious rat that was still hiding somewhere behind the coffee machine.

No, it was the message that bothered him. Taped to the top of the biscuit tin was a piece of paper with the words '*Please look after this rat*'.

And Sergeant Palmer recognized the handwriting.

There was no doubt about it. It was definitely the same.

Chapter Eight
FREE TIME

The next day, Bernard took Karen round to meet Aunt Bee and the two children sat cross-legged on the end of her bed, eating slices of a cake Mrs Donaldson had made, and talking about the watch.

Karen was more curious than Bernard had ever been to know where it had come from, how it might work, and who had made it, but Aunt Bee could tell her very little. She knew no more about the watch than she had already told Bernard, and the conversation eventually turned instead to what you could do with it when you had it.

For Bernard, it was a particular pleasure to share with his friend some of the things he had done over the last few weeks and the difference the watch had made to his life.

He told Karen how he used it to do his schoolwork, to look up answers to questions in class, and to give himself more time if he needed it. He told her what had really happened on the day they went to Portsmouth, and what he had done to the Ryan twins, and how he had used the watch to catch the rat for her birthday.

He also told her how he used the watch when he was playing football and explained that it was the perfect way to win at almost any game.

'It works whatever you're playing,' he said enthusiastically. 'Like, if it's a dice game, you wait till the dice has almost landed, stop time, and then turn it to whatever number you need. Or if it's cards, you can press the watch, look at what the other person's got, give yourself some new ones if you need them. You can't lose!'

'No,' said Karen, who remembered a game of Pelmanism the week before which Bernard had won spectacularly. 'But isn't it cheating?'

'Of course it's cheating!' Bernard agreed. 'But who's going to find out?'

Aunt Bee said she had once used the watch to beat Fred Perry, the great Wimbledon champion, in a tennis match in 1938.

'Tennis?' Bernard was puzzled. 'But didn't he think it was a bit odd? That you were running round the court with a watch in one hand?'

'No, no, my husband held the watch.' Aunt Bee explained. 'I didn't know he was doing it. I was playing my normal game, but if I hit a ball and it was going into the net, he'd stop time and move it. Put the ball a few inches higher or something, you see. Anyway, he made sure whatever I did, the ball always landed in the right place –' she laughed as she remembered – 'and sometimes he moved the ball just when Fred was going to hit it, so that he'd miss. He got terribly cross.'

'But if Bernard uses the watch to win at football,' said Karen, 'what happens if he grows up and uses it to play for Manchester United and then for England and we win the World Cup or something? It wouldn't be fair, would it?'

Bernard stared at her. Winning the World Cup was such an obvious and brilliant idea, he was surprised he had not thought of it himself.

Aunt Bee did not seem to think that using the watch to win at football was very important. When Karen asked her again if she didn't think it would be unfair, the old lady only shrugged and said that, as it was probably the only way England ever would win the World Cup, it might not be such a bad thing.

Karen was not entirely convinced, but if she thought Bernard ought not to use the watch to win at games, she soon forgave him. It was very hard not to forgive someone who shared all his time with you. Especially when he had so much time to share.

And besides, she would have forgiven him anything after the accident.

The accident happened or, more exactly, didn't happen on the following Sunday at the end of half-term. Aunt Bee had been told by the doctor that she must rest as much as possible and Mrs Hewitt had offered to look after Bernard during the day. She told

Mr Beasley that, as she was already looking after Karen, one more wouldn't make any difference.

On Sunday, she had promised to look after Bernard from eleven o'clock so that Mr Beasley could go to Southampton to see a man about buying a lorry. At ten-past, when she had still not returned from the supermarket, Mr Beasley decided he could not wait any longer. Mrs Hewitt was turning into the road when she saw him getting into his car ahead of them. She told Karen to run over, apologize for being late, and find out where Bernard was.

Karen got out of the car, ran to Mr Beasley's Jaguar and pulled open the passenger door.

'I'm sorry we're late,' she said. 'Mum wants to know if you still want her to look after Bernard?'

'Yes, please.' Mr Beasley was already turning the key in the ignition. 'I've left him in his room. Tell your mother I'll be back about four, OK?'

Karen closed the door as Mr Beasley put the car into reverse and it was only as he started driving away, that she realized that her dress was caught in it. She called to Mr Beasley to wait, but he was looking the other way to see if the road was clear and the noise of the engine drowned her words.

Mrs Hewitt saw what was happening and instantly realized the danger. She was out of her car, running down the pavement, shouting at Mr Beasley to stop, but he did not see her. He was looking up the road and wondering whether, if he pulled out fast enough, he could be out into the traffic before an approaching car had reached him.

As the Jaguar reversed into the road, Karen was forced to go with it. For a moment, she managed to run and keep up, and with one hand tried to bang on the window, but then she slipped, and found herself being pulled along the tarmac. Mrs Hewitt saw her fall and ran out from the pavement, directly in the path of the reversing car, screaming at Mr Beasley to stop.

At the last moment, Mr Beasley glanced in his rear-view mirror and realized what was happening. He immediately pulled his foot off the accelerator and moved it to the brake, but even as he did it he knew it was too late. He would never be able to stop the car in time and there was nothing he could do. There was nothing anybody could do.

And there would indeed have been a terrible accident if Karen, as her feet slid inexorably under the car, had not called out to the one person she knew might be able to help.

'Bernard!' she screamed. 'Bernaaaaaaaard!'

Up in his bedroom, Bernard walked to the window and looked out. He had pressed the watch as soon as he had heard Karen's scream – it was an instinctive reaction to any crisis – and he could see at once that something was wrong.

When he came out of the house and walked down to the pavement, he found he had pressed the watch just in time. Karen, with one hand on the door handle, was being dragged along the ground and her right leg was within centimetres of being run over by the front wheel. Mr Beasley, in the driving seat, had just realized what was happening and his eyes were wide with horror as he looked in the mirror. Behind him, Mrs Hewitt was standing directly in the path of the car with her eyes tightly closed. She had her hands held out in front of her and her mouth open as she screamed at Mr Beasley to stop.

Bernard set about putting things to rights. He began by opening the car door to release Karen's dress, then swung her upright, and lifted her back and out of the way on to the pavement.

He moved Mrs Hewitt, who was rather taller and heavier, in a slightly different way. He pushed the top part of her body backwards until she was leaning at an angle of about forty-five degrees. He lifted her feet off the ground until she was horizontal to the road, then he pushed her towards the pavement before reversing the process so that she was standing upright again, but no longer in the path of the car.

Finally, he opened the driver's door of his father's car, checked his seat belt was properly done up, turned off the ignition and put on the handbrake. Then he went back to the garden gate and started time again.

For a moment, there was a great deal of noise. Karen was still screaming for Bernard, Mrs Hewitt was screaming at Mr Beasley, the car engine was revving – and then everything went quiet. Both Karen and Mrs Hewitt realized they were standing safely out of harm's way, the car jolted to a halt and the engine died.

Bernard stepped over to Karen.

'Are you all right?'

'I'll tell you in a minute,' she said.

He looked at Mrs Hewitt. 'Everything OK?'

'I . . . I . . .' Mrs Hewitt was trying to come to terms with the fact that one moment ago both she and her daughter had been on the point of being killed but that now everything seemed to be all right.

'Yes, I'm fine, Bernard,' she said, eventually. 'Thank you.'

Mr Beasley had got out of the car and was standing in the road, his face drained of blood, staring first at Karen and then at her mother.

Bernard went over to him.

'If you drive the car back to the kerb, Dad,' he said, 'I think we should get Mrs Hewitt inside to sit down for a bit, don't you?'

Mr Beasley thought sitting down somewhere was a very good idea. At least until his legs had stopped shaking.

In the Hewitt's kitchen, as Bernard poured more hot water into the teapot, Karen's mother recovered quite rapidly. In her mind, she had already decided that she must have imagined the whole thing. She had, after all, had her eyes closed a lot of the time. Mr Beasley must have seen what was happening and stopped. It was as simple as that, and she felt rather embarrassed at the way she had screamed at him.

'I thought maybe you should have some sugar.'

Bernard put a large mug of tea on the table in front of his father and a sugar bowl. 'I read in a book once that it's good for shock.'

Mr Beasley had not spoken since he came in. He was not finding it as easy as his neighbour to accept what had happened outside. In his rear-view mirror, he knew, he had seen Mrs Hewitt barely a foot away from the back of the car. At the same time he had seen, out of the corner of his eye, Karen's face disappearing below the window and part of her dress clearly caught in the door. He had known, even as he moved his foot to the brake, that there was no chance of stopping before he ran over them both and yet . . . and yet they had not been run over.

And his car had somehow stopped.

Mr Beasley did not know how the car engine had been turned off or handbrake put on, but he did know he had been extremely lucky. What on earth had he been doing hurrying to pull out into the road like that? Why hadn't he waited till he knew the road was clear? Why did he think it was so important to get to Southampton today anyway? What was the hurry? Why was he *always* hurrying? Why . . .?

His eyes travelled round the meticulously tidy kitchen to Bernard, who was pouring a glass of milk for Karen and another for himself. He seemed to have taken charge of everything. He had brought them all inside, sat them down, made the tea . . . And, looking at his son, Mr Beasley wondered when this quietly confident young lad had taken over from the little boy who always looked so worried about everything. When had that happened? And why hadn't he noticed it before?

'I'm sorry I screamed at you like that.' Mrs Hewitt was talking to him. 'Only I thought you weren't going to stop. I feel so silly. And I'm afraid we've upset all your plans for going out.'

'No,' Mr Beasley finally spoke. 'No, that's all right. It wasn't important. And I've changed my mind. I'm not going anywhere today.'

What he needed, Mr Beasley decided, was somewhere quiet where he could sit down and do some serious thinking.

Because his aunt was not supposed to get out of bed, it was Bernard who set the moth trap in the evenings and, the following morning, brought in the insects that had been caught. That evening, in the fading light, he carried the wooden box down the garden to its place between the apple trees, plugged the mercury vapour lamp into the extension lead, and turned it on. In the night, the moths would be attracted to the light and the next morning he and his aunt would count how many there were and what type.

When he came back into the house, he found Karen pouring a measure of iron tonic into two plastic medicine cups.

'Your aunt says we need to take some of this every day –' she passed one of the cups to Bernard – 'otherwise we'll get ill.'

'I thought it was best if she knew,' said Aunt Bee. 'I hope you don't mind.'

'Not at all.' Bernard took the cup and drank. 'I was thinking the same thing myself.'

'And Karen's been telling me –' Aunt Bee pulled herself up on the pillows – 'what happened this morning. She says you saved her life.'

'And he was so calm about it!' Karen spoke before Bernard could reply. 'You should have seen him, Aunt Bee. The rest of us were frightened out of our wits, but he wasn't bothered at all.'

'Well,' said Bernard modestly, 'there's nothing to be bothered about when you've got the watch, is there?' And, as he said it, he understood it was no more than the truth.

When he had the watch, he was never worried or frightened. There had been a time, not so long ago, when he had been worried and frightened a good deal of the time – as a lot of people are. He had been worried about being late for school, frightened of what people might say if he did his work wrong, worried about not being able to do what he was asked ... But since Aunt Bee had given him the watch, all that had gone.

Of all the things the watch had done for him, he suddenly realized, this was by far the most important. It might be fun to be good in class, to have the time to do the things he wanted, to be a brilliant goalkeeper, even to be a hero and save people's lives – but better than any of these was the freedom from fear.

It was as if fear was something you could only feel in time. Fear was, after all, the feeling that you might lose something and you could only lose things in time. Only time took things away. Only in time could you be hurt. Only in time could the bad things happen and, if you could stop time, you could stop the bad things too.

'When you've got this,' he said, holding the watch, 'you don't have to be frightened of anything, do you?'

'Nearly anything.' Aunt Bee spoke very gently. 'Nearly anything.'

Mr Beasley sat at the desk in his front room. He had been sitting there most of the day, staring out over the front garden to the road, and thinking. It was getting dark now, but he had not turned on the light.

He had thought about many things. He had thought about Bernard, and how strange it was that you could live in the same house as someone and not notice how quickly they were growing up. He thought about his business and why he worked so hard. He thought about Mrs Hewitt, living next door in that neat little flat with everything so carefully arranged and organized. And he thought about his own house, with the piles of dusty files that littered the floor behind him and the kitchen with its empty fridge and its stack of dirty dishes in the sink.

And he thought about Aunt Bee and about moths. He wasn't quite sure where the moths came into it, but he still thought about them. They seemed to be part of the pattern.

Mr Beasley knew he was not clever in the way that

some people are. He had never passed an exam in his life, but when he had a problem, he faced it with a formidable determination and persistence. He had decided that morning that he had a problem and, after worrying at it for nearly six hours, he thought he had come up with a possible solution. Slowly, he got to his feet and went next door to see Mrs Hewitt.

'I've been thinking,' he said, when Mrs Hewitt had sat him down in her living room, 'that I've been making a mistake. With my work.'

Mrs Hewitt had a rough idea how much money Mr Beasley made from his business and thought she could do with making a few mistakes like that herself. But she didn't say anything.

'I should have realized ages ago,' Mr Beasley continued. 'I'm not cut out to do paperwork. I did it to start with because there wasn't anyone else, and it kept me busy at weekends, but it's not what I'm good at. Never have been. What I need is someone to help do that bit for me, and I was wondering if you'd be interested.'

'Me?' Mrs Hewitt stared at him. 'You want me to help with your paperwork?'

'Yes,' said Mr Beasley.

'But I don't have any qualifications.'

'It's mostly common sense, and being organized,' said Mr Beasley. 'You'd be surprised how much of running a business is common sense and being organized. I'd pay you, of course.'

He mentioned an hourly rate that was about five times what Mrs Hewitt earned at the card shop.

'Oh,' she gulped. 'Well, that sounds very reasonable.'

'I know you can't do it full time,' Mr Beasley explained. 'But it's the sort of thing you could do pretty much when you liked. Daytime, evenings, weekends.'

'In the holidays I have Karen to look after,' said Mrs Hewitt, 'and while your aunt's ill there's Bernard too . . .'

'Well, that's part of the point, really.' Mr Beasley looked carefully at his shoes. 'You see, if you were doing the paperwork, I thought maybe I could take a turn with the children. Take them off to a movie or a football match or something. If Karen didn't mind.'

For a moment, Mrs Hewitt was too astonished to speak.

'You don't have to decide now, of course, but perhaps you'll think it over, eh? And if you thought you might be interested, you could come next door, look at some of the papers and –'

'Well, I'm not doing anything much at the moment,' Mrs Hewitt stood up. 'Why don't I come and have a look at them now?'

'Oh. Right. OK, then!'

Mr Beasley walked with her to the door. Outside, it was one of those clear sunny evenings that gave the first faint promise of spring. There was even a breath of warmth in the air and he noticed that the crocuses, neatly planted in Mrs Hewitt's garden, were coming into flower.

As he led her up the steps to his own house, there

flashed into his mind's eye a picture of a moth, pausing in its flight for a moment before changing direction and heading south, towards the sun.

Chapter Nine

TIME OUT

Ten days later, Aunt Bee was taken into hospital.

It was the Wednesday of the finals of the football competition. Bernard's father had taken the afternoon off work to come and watch, and it looked as if half the town had done the same. Mr Tree had cancelled all the afternoon lessons and the entire school, including the staff, crossed the road to the playing fields to join the parents and supporters on the touchline.

It was an exciting game, and Karen was probably the only spectator who knew there was never really any doubt who would win. With Bernard in goal, attack after attack was confidently beaten off and in the second half Louis Hugh-Jones, who was turning into an astonishingly effective striker, scored three goals for the school. On the touchline, Mr Beasley, who had never seen his son play before, watched the whole thing in astonishment.

'He's quite good, isn't he?' he told Mr Tree, standing beside him. 'I'd no idea.'

'Bernard? Oh yes!' The headmaster nodded vigorously. 'A remarkable find. Miss Picot reckons he'll be playing for England one day.'

'He won't really, will he?' asked Karen, standing with her mother, the other side of Mr Beasley.

'Miss Picot's very serious about it,' said Mr Tree. 'She says it's only a question of time.'

At the end of the match, amid tremendous cheers for the winners, everyone went back to the school for the presentation of the cup and an enormous tea generously provided, the headmaster said, by a local businessman, whom Bernard later found was his father.

And when it was time to go home, Bernard, Karen, Mr Beasley and Mrs Hewitt all went round to Aunt Bee's so that Bernard could show her the silver trophy, which he had been allowed to keep until the following day when it would go on display in the cupboard in the main school hall.

They pushed open the door to Aunt Bee's house, singing 'We won the cup!' and with Bernard triumphantly waving the trophy above his head, to find Aunt Bee lying on the carpet in front of the fireplace, crumpled up like a piece of old cloth.

It looked as if she had got out bed, probably to put some more coal on the fire, and collapsed. At first, Bernard thought she was dead, but Mrs Hewitt said she was still breathing and Mr Beasley rang for the emergency services.

As they waited for the ambulance to arrive, Bernard remembered how his aunt had corrected him when he said that, with the watch, you need no longer be frightened of anything.

He had the watch with him now but, as the men in green overalls lifted Aunt Bee on to a stretcher and took her outside, he felt more worried and frightened than he could remember.

Everyone told Bernard there was no need to worry. They said the doctors and nurses at the hospital would find out what was wrong with his aunt and soon put it right. But it didn't stop him worrying.

Each day, his father took him to visit her at the hospital, but each day Aunt Bee looked exactly the same. She lay in the bed, not moving, not speaking and hardly breathing so that you would notice. Some days, he was not even allowed to see her. With the watch, of course, he could ignore this and, in frozen time, he would go into her room and leave a bunch of flowers and maybe a note on her bedside table, telling her any new adventures he and Karen had had with the watch – and about the moths.

Looking after the moth records was the one thing that Bernard knew his aunt would want him to do while she was away. Three times a week, he went down to her house in the evening and set the trap in its place between the apple trees. He noted down the temperature and whether the sky was cloudy or clear, and the next morning went back and carefully recorded the numbers and breeds of moths caught in the box, before releasing them.

He wanted very much for his aunt to get better and come home. It was a time when everything else in his life was going so well. He was enjoying . . . everything. At school, he and Karen were always top of the class. At home, thanks to Mrs Hewitt's help with the paperwork, his father had had time to take them to the cinema and bowling. And sharing the watch with Karen, Bernard had found, was even more fun than having it on his own.

They were always together, passing the watch between them as they needed it. They sat together in class, did their work together and, after school, would walk into town together to explore the shops. One of Karen's favourite occupations was using the watch to try on clothes without any shop assistants coming over to ask if she was going to buy anything.

Life was good. In fact, it was very good. And if only his aunt would get better, Bernard thought, it would be more than very good, it would be perfect.

One morning, when Aunt Bee had been in hospital for a little over a week, Bernard was collecting the moths from the trap with his father, who had come along to watch. There were a larger number of insects than usual as the weather had been mild, and Bernard was in the process of explaining to Mr Beasley the difference between a Small and a Common Quaker, when Mrs Donaldson emerged from the house.

'I'm sorry to disturb you, Mr Beasley.' There was a worried look on her face as she walked down from the house, panting slightly for breath. 'But I wonder if you could help me?'

'Of course.' Mr Beasley stood up. 'What is it?'

'As you know, I'm sort of looking after Mrs Temperley's house while she's . . . indisposed.' Mrs Donaldson mopped her forehead with a handkerchief. 'And I'm sure you know she has some rather valuable items.'

'Yes?' Mr Beasley frowned. 'Why? Is something missing?'

'She had a watch,' said Mrs Donaldson. 'A gold pocket watch. She was never without it. And I've searched high and low but there's not a trace of it anywhere.'

'Oh, that's all right.' Mr Beasley relaxed. 'Bernard's got it. She lent it to him.'

'Oh, that is relief!' Mrs Donaldson turned to Bernard. 'Only she was quite agitated last night when I told her I hadn't been able to find it. She'll be so pleased.'

'She's talking again?' asked Mr Beasley.

'In snatches.' Mrs Donaldson gave a vague wave of her arm. 'She's still unconscious most of the time, but she did particularly ask me to bring in the watch.' She paused and looked at Bernard again. 'I'm taking some clean clothes in for her this morning. Perhaps I could take the watch in for her as well?'

If his aunt wanted the watch, Bernard thought,

the sooner she had it the better, but she had always told him how important it was to keep it away from other people.

'That's very kind of you,' he said, 'but I'm going in with Dad after tea. I'll give it to her then.'

'Yes, of course.' Mrs Donaldson nodded. 'That'd be best. And I'll tell her when I go in that's what you're doing, so she doesn't have to worry.' She hesitated. 'We are talking about the same watch, are we? I mean, do you have it with you? Could I see it?'

The chain of the watch hung from Bernard's button down to his pocket so it was quite clear he had it with him. With an odd feeling of reluctance, he took it from his pocket and held it out.

Mrs Donaldson leant forward. 'Oh yes! That looks like the one. And on the other side?' She reached out with a finger and thumb and turned the watch over.

It happened so quickly that it was done before Bernard had even realized the danger. And by the time he had, it was too late.

Mrs Donaldson withdrew her hand as if nothing had happened. 'Oh yes! It's beautiful, isn't it?' As she smiled at Bernard, there was a gleam of triumph in her eyes. 'Take care of it, won't you?'

Bernard said nothing. He was too shocked to speak.

'Well, I must get back to work.' Mrs Donaldson turned back to the house. 'Thank you both so much. And I'll let Mrs Temperley know that you'll be in later and that there's nothing to worry about.'

'Well, that's wonderful news about Aunt Bee talking again, isn't it?' Mr Beasley smiled happily at his son. 'Very good news.'

Bernard did not reply. He had not moved since Mrs Donaldson had touched the watch that he still held in his hand. Only as he watched her disappear into the house did he look down and gently press the button with his thumb.

But he already knew what would happen.

Nothing.

Nothing at all.

'You mean it's not working?' asked Karen.

'I mean it's not the same watch.' Bernard passed it across. He had walked home with his father, who was now downstairs with Mrs Hewitt working on his VAT return. 'Here. See for yourself.'

Karen took the watch and knew instantly that Bernard was right. The watch might look the same, but it felt quite different. It was not as heavy and lacked that curious resistance to movement that made holding it such a strange sensation.

'You mean she changed it? But how could she? You said she barely touched it. And you and your dad were both watching.'

'It doesn't matter who was watching, does it?' said Bernard. 'All she had to do was press the button. Then, in frozen time, she could unclip the real watch from the chain, put that one on instead, start time again and carry on as if nothing had happened.'

'But . . . but it looks exactly the same.' Karen stared at the watch in her hand. 'How could she get one that looked exactly the same?'

'Aunt Bee had a copy. Maybe she stole it from her. Maybe she went to a shop and found one that looked the same. Or made one. She had enough time.'

Bernard was furious with himself for being fooled so easily. It had never even occurred to him that Mrs Donaldson might know what the watch did. Thinking back, he realized there were plenty of ways she might have found out. She could have overheard him talking to Aunt Bee, or with Karen in the garden, or read the notes he left at the hospital.

'Mrs Donaldson . . .' Karen shook her head. 'I can't believe it. She was always so nice.'

'Aunt Bee said the watch could make even the nicest people behave strangely.'

Bernard stared gloomily at the carpet. Two things worried him almost as much as losing the watch. First, how was he ever going to explain to Aunt Bee that he could not give back her watch because he no longer had it? And secondly, what exactly was Mrs Donaldson planning to do with it?

He had a nasty feeling it that it would not be long before he found out.

Sergeant Palmer took off his helmet and rubbed thoughtfully at the back of his neck.

'Right,' he said. 'Let's go through it all again, shall we? You opened the safe at about eleven . . .'

'At exactly eleven o'clock.' Mr Lilac, the bank's deputy manager, swallowed nervously before speaking. 'That's when the time lock turned off. I punched in the combination, Derek here turned the windlass, and when he pulled open the door, I went in.'

'And when you came into the safe, the money was still here?'

'Yes!' Mr Lilac nodded vigorously. 'It was stacked on all these shelves.'

'About seven hundred and forty-nine thousand pounds?'

'Yes.' Mr Lilac gulped.

'But when Derek came in –' Sergeant Palmer gestured to the young man beside him – 'the shelves were empty.'

'It disappeared!' Mr Lilac was close to tears. 'I promise you! The money was here when I came in then it . . . it disappeared! You have to believe me!'

The funny thing was, thought Sergeant Palmer, that he did believe him. Only an hour before, he had heard an almost identical story from the manager of Solitaire, the jeweller's at the top of the High Street. Mr Knapps said he had opened a glass security door to make an adjustment to the display in one of his cabinets, when the entire contents of the shelves had disappeared. One second they were there, he claimed, and then they were gone. No one else had been in the shop. A hundred thousand pounds' worth of jewellery had simply vanished out of existence. Sergeant Palmer knew Mr Knapps well, and knew that if he had suddenly decided to steal his own stock he would have thought up a much better story than that.

A police constable stepped into the bank safe and handed Sergeant Palmer a note. It said that three valuable paintings by an artist called S. L. Lowry had disappeared from the collection on display in the Guildhall.

Sergeant Palmer sighed again. His board for promotion to Inspector was in four days' time and a crime wave of this dimension, right on his own patch, was the last thing he needed.

The city's crime wave was on the national news that evening. Bernard and Karen watched it on the television in Bernard's bedroom. As well as the bank, the jeweller's and the paintings from the art exhibition, someone had taken nineteen pairs of shoes from Russell and Bromley's, five-and-a-half thousand pounds' worth of designer clothes from a dress shop called Oasis and seventy-two bottles of champagne from Oddbins.

'You think they were all her?' said Karen.

Bernard nodded. 'Looks like it.'

'What are you going to tell your aunt?'

Bernard had no idea what he would tell Aunt Bee, but that at least was no longer an immediate problem. Mr Beasley had rung the ward at four o'clock and the staff nurse said that Aunt Bee was not well enough to receive visitors that day.

'Not much point going out there, if they won't let

us see her,' he told Bernard. 'How about we take her some flowers after lunch tomorrow?'

Downstairs, Mr Beasley was whistling cheerily as he bustled round the kitchen, preparing the ingredients to make a risotto. He could not help but be cheerful when he thought of the difference Mrs Hewitt had made to the room next door. In the last two and a half weeks, the letters, receipts and invoices that had once littered the floor had been miraculously transformed into neat piles, with names and dates neatly written on the neatly stacked folders that held them. Filing cabinets had appeared. And the VAT form, which usually took him several weekends to complete, was already sitting with its envelope on the desk, ready to be sent off in the morning.

His only concern was that Mrs Hewitt was driving herself too hard. In fact, she was still working there now, which was why he had offered to cook supper for them all. Mr Beasley was a good cook. It was not something he had bothered with in recent years – it had never seemed worth it, just for Bernard and himself – but now he rather enjoyed the prospect of producing a proper meal for the four of them.

As he measured out the rice into the pan, he not only whistled, he sang.

Upstairs, Bernard switched off the television and turned to Karen.

'We can't just sit here and not do anything!' he said. 'We have to stop her.'

'How can we?' Karen was lying on the bed, staring

at the ceiling. 'If someone's got the watch, you can't get near them, can you? Unless they let you. All they have to do is press the button and they're somewhere else.'

'But she's using the watch to steal everything!' said Bernard. 'If we went round to where she lives, maybe we could find some of it and –'

'I think we need to keep away from Mrs Donaldson,' Karen interrupted him. 'Well away. You said yourself, the one chance we have of getting the watch back is to wait and that's what we have to do. We have to wait.'

Neither of them knew how long it might take. With luck, it would be no more than two or three days, but until then, Karen insisted, the further they kept from Mrs Donaldson the better.

She was an imaginative as well as an intelligent girl and she had already worked out that there were much worse things than burglaries Mrs Donaldson could do with the watch if she put her mind to it.

Much worse.

And the further they kept away from her the better.

Chapter Ten
LOST TIME

Although the last thing the children had wanted, in the short term, was to see Mrs Donaldson again, they met her the next morning.

It was a Sunday and Bernard and Karen were leaving Aunt Bee's house after emptying the moth trap, when a large, metallic-blue Mercedes convertible drew up at the pavement and Mrs Donaldson got out. She was wearing a silk suit, an enormous ring of pearls, a gold brooch and diamond earrings.

'Well, well, well! Just the people I needed to see. No, no, don't go away!' The children had been backing towards the gate. 'Let's all go indoors and have a little talk, shall we?'

Tottering slightly in her high-heeled shoes and with a bottle of champagne tucked under one arm, she made her way up the steps to Aunt Bee's front door.

'Come along!' She called back to the children as she fumbled in a pocket of her coat for a key. 'It won't take long, I promise. Hardly any time at all!'

'You think it's safe to go in with her?' Bernard whispered.

'No,' said Karen, 'but I don't think we have a choice.'

Inside, Aunt Bee's drawing room looked as if a bomb had hit it. There were clothes draped over the furniture, glasses and empty bottles covered the mantelpiece and it was almost impossible to walk because of the boxes of shoes that littered the floor. On one of the sofas lay an open suitcase full of money.

'Not bad for one day's work, eh?' Mrs Donaldson had opened the bottle of champagne and was pouring herself a drink. 'Don't worry. I'm not going to be here long, but I needed somewhere to keep all this till I get a place of my own.' She took a sip of her drink. 'You had the watch for over a month, didn't you, Bernard? And what did you manage to do? Play a few tricks on the teachers or something?'

'You can't use it for stealing things.' Bernard was staring round the room in horror. 'That's not what it's for!'

'Ah! Now I'm glad you said that –' Mrs Donaldson put down her glass – 'because that's what I want you both to understand. All this –' she gestured round the room – 'is *exactly* what the watch is for, because the watch is for doing what *I* want. Do you see?'

Mrs Donaldson was still smiling, but the smile was not a pleasant one. With every passing second, she looked less and less like the woman who had cooked and cleaned for Bernard's aunt.

'While I have the watch, I can do whatever I want. And nobody can take it from me because, wherever you think I am . . .'

Quite suddenly, Mrs Donaldson vanished from the room, but her voice continued from somewhere out in the hall. 'In no time at all, I can be somewhere else.'

Her head appeared for a moment round the door to the hall and promptly vanished again.

'Usually somewhere rather surprising.' This time the voice came from right behind them, making both children jump.

'So, I'll tell you what's going to happen.' She put a large hand on Bernard's shoulder and another on Karen's. 'You're both going to forget you ever saw the watch. If your aunt asks if you've still got it, you show her the other one and say yes. And then you forget about everything, OK?' Her face was very close to Bernard's and he could feel her breath, hot on his cheek. 'Because if you don't, things can happen. They can happen to your friend here . . .'

Bernard suddenly realized that Karen was no longer standing beside him. In fact, she was no longer anywhere in the room.

'Or they can happen to you.' Mrs Donaldson was still standing behind him. 'You want to remember that.'

'Yes,' said Bernard. 'Where's Karen?'

'Don't worry, she's all right. For the moment. But remember, Bernard, while I have the watch, I can do anything.'

'Please,' said Bernard, 'Tell me where Karen –'

He got no further. He was no longer standing in his aunt's drawing room, but somewhere in the middle of the road outside and a bus was driving straight towards him. He saw the driver's eyes open wide in horror, heard him slam on the brakes and then, just as the bus was about to hit him . . .

He was standing on the parapet of the bridge that ran over the river at the bottom of the High Street. Ten metres below, the water swirled blackly round one of the piers and he felt a hand push him in the small of the back so that he fell forward and . . .

He was standing on the railway line in between the platforms at the station. In the distance, he could hear the two-tone whoop of a diesel train approaching. He opened his mouth to scream when . . .

He was back in his aunt's drawing room again, sitting on a chair, while Mrs Donaldson stood at the fireplace holding her drink in one hand and the watch in the other.

'You see, Bernard?' she said. 'I can come out of nowhere, pick you up, and put you wherever I like. You and your friend. Best not to do anything to annoy me. You follow?'

'Yes. Yes, I do,' said Bernard. 'Where's Karen? Please?'

'She's outside. Here.' Mrs Donaldson produced a pair of scissors. 'You'll need these.'

Bernard found Karen sitting on the steps outside the front door. She didn't say anything when he sat down beside her because she had a big strip of sticky tape over her mouth. There was more tape wrapped round her ankles and her wrists under her coat. Bernard cut her free with the scissors.

'Are you all right?'

Karen nodded. 'I don't think she'd have done anything really,' she said, eventually. 'She just wanted to frighten us.'

'You reckon?' said Bernard. 'Well, it certainly worked on me.'

Mr Beasley put down the phone in the kitchen, and walked thoughtfully over to the window, wondering what to do.

From the room next door, he could hear the sound of a filing cabinet being opened and closed. Mrs Hewitt was going through his garage invoices. That morning, she had found a four-figure bill that he appeared to have paid twice and she was checking that this was a mistake that had been made only once.

Mr Beasley sighed. His phone call had been from the hospital and he was wondering if he should tell Bernard about it. Normally, he would not have hesitated but, in this case, he thought it might be better to say nothing. At least for the moment.

When Bernard had returned an hour or so before,

he had looked so pale and worried that Mr Beasley had thought perhaps he was going down with more of whatever had landed him in hospital that last time. But then he reminded himself that Bernard had good reason for looking pale and worried. He was very close to his aunt and of course he missed her and was worried for her. Why shouldn't he be? Come to that, he was worried enough himself.

There was plenty to worry about. When the nurse rang from the hospital, it had not been good news.

Not good news at all.

Up in his bedroom, Bernard found that the more he thought about what had happened that morning, the more frightened he became. Moving Karen in frozen time to prevent her being run over was one thing; the idea that someone else could use the same technique to move him into the path of a passing bus was quite another.

The power of the watch for harm was almost too awful to think about. Even talking about what they might do to try and get it back was, Karen pointed out, extremely dangerous. If Mrs Donaldson was suspicious and wanted to know if they were planning anything, she could use the watch to hide in his bedroom wardrobe or be standing at this very moment outside on the landing to listen. She could have set a tape recorder going under the bed, she could have . . .

The point was that, with the watch, she could do anything.

The only thing to do was wait. They both knew that, as long as Mrs Donaldson did not know that the watch used up the iron in her body, then at some stage she was going to pass out in exactly the way Bernard had in the back of Mrs Hewitt's car. When she did, they would have their one chance to act.

But how long would it take? It had been three days before Bernard fell ill. Would it take more time with an older person, or less? And when it did happen, how would they know? And even if they knew, what exactly should they do?

At the moment, the only thing Bernard was sure of was that Karen had been right and that they needed to stay as far away from Mrs Donaldson as possible.

'Mind you, it's not going to be easy.' Karen was standing at the window and now pointed down the road. 'Look.'

'What is it?' Bernard leapt to his feet and joined her at the window in time to see the blue Mercedes draw up outside and Mrs Donaldson get out and walk up the path to the house.

She was back.

Mrs Hewitt had enjoyed her morning. It was the sort of work that many people might have found tedious or difficult, but not her. She had the sort of tidy, precise mind that found bringing order and system to the chaos of Mr Beasley's paperwork deeply satisfying.

And now she had discovered two more examples

of John's garage charging him twice for the same work. Once might be a mistake, but this looked like deliberate fraud. The trouble was, if you didn't have a proper filing system it was so easy for these people to take advantage of you.

She was on her way to the kitchen to show Mr Beasley the bills when the front-door bell rang.

'It's all right,' she called. 'I'll get it.'

She opened the front door, and it was a moment before she recognized the bejewelled figure on the step.

'Mrs Donaldson?'

'I'm sorry to disturb you.' Mrs Donaldson wrenched her mouth into a smile. 'But could I have a word with Bernard?'

'Yes, of course.' Mrs Hewitt stepped back to let Mrs Donaldson into the hall. 'He was out with Karen earlier, but I think he's back.' She called up the stairs. 'Bernard? Oh, there you are!'

Bernard was already coming down, while Karen hovered on the landing.

'Ah, Bernard!' Mrs Donaldson walked towards him. 'I'll need the key, won't I?'

'The what?'

'The key, Bernard.' She was holding the watch in one hand and was no longer making any effort to smile. 'I want the key. Now.'

'I don't know what you're talking about.' If Bernard had had a key, any key, he would have given it to Mrs Donaldson immediately. The sight of her, with a thumb poised over the button of the watch, was terrifying enough to make him do whatever she wanted.

'Don't mess with me, laddy.' Mrs Donaldson's eyes narrowed. 'I warned you what happens to people who mess with me.'

'Mrs Donaldson, please! You're frightening the boy!' Mrs Hewitt came to stand beside Bernard, visibly shocked at the way Aunt Bee's cleaning lady was behaving.

'She gave you the watch.' Mrs Donaldson stared fixedly at Bernard. 'She wouldn't have given you the watch without the key. Where is it?'

'The watch doesn't have a key!' said Bernard, desperately. 'It just goes.'

'You give me the key, you little brat or I'll –'

'No!' As Mrs Donaldson grabbed the front of Bernard's shirt and raised an arm to hit him, Mrs Hewitt stepped defiantly between them.

'Leave him alone,' she pleaded. 'For goodness' sake, he's a child!'

Mrs Donaldson swung a fist to knock her out of the way, but the blow never landed.

Instead, she found her arm in the remarkably powerful grip of Mr Beasley, who had emerged from the kitchen.

'We'll have none of that in this house, if you don't mind.' Mr Beasley spoke with the easy confidence of a man who has broken up fights in lorry parks across most of Europe. 'What's all this about?'

'You let go of me or you'll regret it!' hissed Mrs Donaldson.

'Please, Dad!' Bernard was more terrified than ever. 'Do what she says. She means it.'

'And so do I.' In one swift move, Mr Beasley pulled Mrs Donaldson's arm behind her back and marched her firmly out of the front door. 'I don't know what's going on, but until you can talk about it in a civilized manner, I'm afraid you'll have to leave.'

Mrs Donaldson was still screaming for the key and waving the watch in her other hand as Mr Beasley forced her down the path to the pavement and Bernard, watching, waited for her to press the button and exact a terrible revenge.

But she didn't. Instead, Mr Beasley walked her all the way back to her blue Mercedes where, without any warning, Mrs Donaldson suddenly collapsed on the pavement.

Mrs Hewitt, watching from the front door, ran down to see what had happened, with Bernard and Karen following close behind.

'She just collapsed!' Mr Beasley stared in some embarrassment at the body on the ground. 'Is she all right?'

'I think so.' Mrs Hewitt could find no trace of an injury. 'But she's unconscious. It's odd. She's like Bernard was that day he passed out in the back of the car. You'd better call an ambulance, John. And, Karen, get me a cushion and a rug from the house. I'll put her in the recovery position.'

While Mr Beasley and Karen ran back to the house, and Mrs Hewitt prepared to move Mrs

Donaldson on to her side, Bernard quietly reached down and retrieved his watch.

He realized as soon as he looked at it why Mrs Donaldson had not used it. The hands pointed to exactly one minute to twelve and they were not moving. When Bernard pressed the button, nothing happened. What Mrs Donaldson had done to it, he had no idea, but one thing was clear.

The watch had stopped and there was only one person Bernard could think of who might know what to do about it.

Chapter Eleven
OUT OF TIME

Sergeant Palmer put three teaspoonfuls of sugar in his mug and stirred it carefully.

'So what happened then?'

'Well,' said Mrs Hewitt, 'then she grabbed Bernard by the front of his shirt, and was going to hit him, and when I got in the way, she was going to hit me, but fortunately John came out and stopped her.'

She smiled gratefully at Mr Beasley, sitting beside her at the kitchen table.

'I said I thought she ought to leave.' Mr Beasley took up the story. 'So I took her outside to the pavement, where she . . . well, she passed out.'

'I see.' Sergeant Palmer sipped his tea. 'And who was it noticed the car?'

'That was Bernard,' said Mr Beasley. 'We were all waiting for the ambulance to arrive and Bernard told me he thought he could see these paintings in the back of Mrs Donaldson's car. I went over . . . and that's when we found everything.'

Sergeant Palmer nodded. He knew exactly what they had found in the blue Mercedes. There were three Lowry paintings, a great many clothes and shoes, several trays of jewellery and a suitcase with something over seven hundred thousand pounds in cash. The Chief Constable would be giving a televised press conference on the discovery in two hour's time, and had asked that Sergeant Palmer be with him.

'Is that your son over there?' He pointed to a photograph on the kitchen dresser.

'Yes, that's Bernard.' Mr Beasley frowned. 'I'm sorry he's not here at the moment. You'll want to talk to him, won't you?'

Sergeant Palmer was only half listening. He had seen the face in the photo before, but for the moment he could not remember where.

'What? Oh, yes. Yes, I will. Mostly to say thank you, of course. I think we owe him that at least. Is he around?'

'No, he's not.' Karen came into the kitchen. 'He's gone to the hospital. He left this note.'

As she gave Mr Beasley Bernard's note, Sergeant Palmer suddenly remembered where he had seen the face in the photo. It was the boy on the bicycle, that day at the roundabout. He was sure of it. He was even wearing the same sweater.

'It looks like he's gone to see his aunt.' Mr Beasley stood up. 'She's been very ill recently, you see, and he . . . Look, I think I'd better go and find him.'

'Before you do . . .' The sergeant leaned across the table. 'Could I see that note, please?'

Sergeant Palmer knew, even before Mr Beasley passed him the note, that he would recognize the handwriting. It was one of those days when the pieces of more than one puzzle seemed to be coming together.

Bernard had known that it would be several hours before his father and Mrs Hewitt had sorted things out with the police about Mrs Donaldson, and he had the feeling that he did not have several hours. It was important, very important, that he get to see Aunt Bee as soon as possible.

He left a note with Karen, telling his father where he was going, and asked her not to give it to him for at least an hour. Then he got his bicycle from the shed at the bottom of the garden and set off for the hospital on his own. He had travelled the route a good many times in the last ten days so he had no trouble finding the way.

Leaving his bicycle by a tree in the hospital car park, he hurried inside, up the stairs to the first floor, and then down the long corridor that led to the ward where Aunt Bee was being looked after. With a gathering sense of urgency, he found himself walking faster and faster until by the end he was running, straight through the reception area and into the room with Aunt Bee's bed.

But Aunt Bee was not there. And while Bernard stared at the large man who now occupied her bed, a harassed young nurse trying to collect up the lunch trays asked him what he was doing.

'I've come to see my aunt,' he explained.

'Visiting doesn't start till two,' said the nurse briskly. 'I'm afraid I'll have to ask you to leave.'

'I can't leave,' said Bernard. 'Not till I've seen my aunt.'

'You can see her at two o'clock.' The nurse took him by the arm and propelled him towards the door. 'I told you, that's when visiting starts. And unaccompanied children are not allowed in the adult wards.'

'Please!' Bernard struggled to pull himself free. 'You have to let me see her. You have to!'

'Is there a problem?' The staff nurse had come out her office. 'Oh, goodness! It's Bernard isn't it? Bernard Beasley?' She turned to the nurse. 'It's all right, I'll look after this.' She smiled cheerfully down at Bernard. 'I don't suppose you know who I am, do you?'

Bernard admitted that he had no idea.

'I'm Mrs Hugh-Jones. My son, Louis, plays in your school football team. I've watched you in goal. You're *very* good!' The staff nurse held out a hand and Bernard shook it. 'What can I do for you?'

'I need to see my aunt,' said Bernard. 'Mrs Beatrice Temperley. It's very important.'

'Ah!' The staff-nurse pursed her lips. 'Well, officially, visiting's not allowed for another hour. But I think we can stretch a point in the circumstances. Do you know where she is?'

'She was in there,' Bernard pointed to the room his aunt had been in, 'but she's not any more.'

'Oh, we move them around all the time.' The staff nurse chuckled. 'Can't let them get too comfortable. I've only just come on duty, so I don't know offhand where they've put her, but we can soon find out.'

She walked over to the reception desk, tapped Mrs Temperley's name into the computer terminal and then stared at the screen.

She stared for some time before eventually looking back at Bernard.

'Is anyone with you?' she asked.

'I came on my own,' said Bernard. 'Have you found out where my aunt is?'

'Your parents are at home, are they?' The staff nurse ignored his question. 'Do they have a telephone?'

'Why?' Bernard could not understand the delay. 'Look, I just want to see Aunt Bee. Only for a few minutes, but it's really important. I have to ask her something. I *have* to.'

'Bernard,' the staff nurse came out from behind the desk and put an arm on his shoulder. 'I'm sorry. If I could take you to your aunt, I would. Really, I would.' She bent down till her face was on a level with his. 'But I can't do anything until your parents get here. Now, if you could give me their telephone number?'

In the kitchen, Mr Beasley put down the phone.

'It was the hospital,' he said, a little unnecessarily. The others had all been listening and had heard most of the conversation.

He stood up.

'I have to get over there. Straightaway.'

As he reached for the car keys, Sergeant Palmer put a restraining hand on his wrist.

'I'm not sure you should do that.'

'What?' Mr Beasley stared at him blankly.

'Never wise to drive when you're upset,' said the policeman. 'How about I get one of my men to take you. In a police car.'

Bernard had no idea what the time was. There was no clock on the wall and Aunt Bee's watch still said it was one minute to twelve.

The staff nurse had asked him to wait in what she called the television room. It was a room containing about a dozen chairs, but no television. He had no idea how long he had been there and was wondering if perhaps he had been forgotten, when the door suddenly swung open.

'Ah, there you are!' Aunt Bee stood in the doorway, smiling brightly. 'I've been looking everywhere for you. I thought maybe you'd gone.'

'Auntie?' Bernard stared at her in astonishment. 'I thought you were ill?'

'Oh, I was!' Aunt Bee came striding over to join him at the window. 'But it's all right. I'm feeling a lot better now.'

She looked a lot better, Bernard thought. She was walking without her stick, without any trace of a limp, and there was a brightness and a sparkle in her eyes.

'Now –' she put an arm on his shoulder – 'mustn't waste time. There are people waiting for me. But I absolutely refused to go without saying goodbye properly, and I need to tell you about the watch.'

She paused, sensing from the look on Bernard's face that something was wrong.

'What is it? What's the matter?'

'The watch is what I came to see you about,' said Bernard. 'It's not working any more.'

'Not working?' Aunt Bee's face frowned in concern. 'Why? What's happened?'

'Mrs Donaldson got hold of it,' Bernard explained. 'She used it to steal things, and when I got it back . . . I think she's broken it.'

He held out the watch, and his aunt took one look at it and laughed.

'No, no! That's not broken! It's stopped!'

She took the watch and held it up, so that the gold glittered in the sunlight. 'You need to wind it up, that's all. It'll be fine then, you'll see. Now . . .' She led Bernard over to a chair, 'I want you to sit down and listen very carefully, because what I'm going to say is important.'

They sat down and Aunt Bee carefully placed the watch back in Bernard's hands.

'You remember when I first gave this to you, you asked what it was for? Well, that's what I want to tell you, because the one thing you need to know, if you're going to use it properly, is what it's for, do you see?'

Bernard was not entirely sure that he did see but,

while he was wondering if he should say so, his aunt continued talking.

'The watch gives you time, and you can use that time for all sorts of things – as you have. You used it to keep out of trouble. Then you started using it for fun. You used it to be good at schoolwork, to win at games, to help people, to help your friend . . . and doing all those things is fine. They're all very good things to do, as long as you don't hurt other people while you're doing them, but none of them is what the watch is *for*, you know? Because what the watch is for –' Aunt Bee held one of his hands very tightly in hers – 'and this is the bit I want you to remember, what the watch is *for*, is learning.'

She looked expectantly into Bernard's face.

'Learning what?' he asked, eventually.

'Exactly!' Aunt Bee banged her fist on his knee as if he had said something tremendously clever. 'That's the first thing you'll need to find out. What you have to learn! And it's not easy. Not easy at all. We're all like the moths when it comes down to it, you see. It's such a little life and we have to try and get it right.' Her face softened and she gently ruffled his hair. 'But you'll do it. I know you will.'

If there had been more time, Bernard would have admitted that he had no idea what his aunt was talking about, but there was something else he needed to say first. Aunt Bee had told him the watch needed winding up, but she had not said what it could be wound up with.

'How do I wind the watch up, Auntie?' he asked.

'Well, with the key, of course!' She was standing up now and she bent down and gave him a swift kiss. 'I must go. You take care. And remember what I said.'

'You're going?' Bernard was rather taken aback. 'Going where? Why?'

'Oh, come on!' His aunt was already at the door and she gave him a teasing smile. 'Haven't you worked it out yet? Clever boy like you?'

And she gave a little wave, pulled open the door, and was gone.

'Hang on!' Bernard hurried after her. 'About the key. Where do I find it?'

'You use the one I gave you!' Aunt Bee was already striding off down the corridor. 'Goodbye, Bernard!'

And a moment later, she was no longer walking, but running, positively running down the corridor like a girl. Her skirt swirled round her knees, her hair glistened in the sunlight, and her feet danced so lightly over the floor that they barely seemed to touch it.

Halfway down the corridor, she turned.

'You know, Bernard? You were right!'

'What?'

'Remember when you said you thought time was a prison?' Aunt Bee laughed, and the laughter echoed off the walls. 'But to be free, Bernard! To be free!'

At the far end of the corridor, at the bottom of the staircase, a young man was waiting. He had crinkly dark hair and a moustache, and when Aunt Bee saw him she gave a little cry of delight. He held his arms wide open to greet her and she ran straight into them, wrapping her arms around his neck, holding him as tightly as she could.

Bernard did not like to interrupt, but there was something important he still needed to know.

'About the key,' he called. 'Are you quite sure you gave it to me?'

Aunt Bee did not reply and he called again, a little louder. 'Auntie?'

But Aunt Bee did not seem to hear. She was gazing deeply into the eyes of the young man as he slowly released her from his arms, took her by the hand, and led her away up the stairs.

The sunlight from the window at the end of the corridor was so bright that it made Bernard's eyes water as he watched. He blinked. And when he opened them again, Aunt Bee had gone.

They trooped into the television room together and you could see that none of them was quite sure who should speak first or what they should say when they did.

The staff nurse stepped to one side, Mrs Hewitt put an arm around Karen, and it was Mr Beasley who came over and sat beside Bernard.

'We've got some rather sad news,' he said, eventually. 'About Aunt Bee.'

'It's all right,' said Bernard. 'I already know. She came and told me.'

Chapter Twelve
STARTING TIME

Inspector Palmer bounced up the steps two at a time and rang the doorbell. Mr Beasley let him into the hall.

'Alison?' he called. 'It's Sergeant Palmer come to –' he stopped, peering at the two silver stars on the shoulder of the policeman's uniform – 'I do apologize. Inspector Palmer! Congratulations!'

'Thank you.' Inspector Palmer smiled modestly. 'One of the rewards of going for your promotion board three days after you've solved a major crime wave.' He turned to Mrs Hewitt as she emerged from the front room. 'I'm not interrupting anything, am I?'

'Not at all.' Mrs Hewitt shook hands. 'We were just putting some of the details of John's business on to the computer. We needed a break.'

'My new financial director! Saved me a fortune already.' Mr Beasley spoke proudly and put an arm round Mrs Hewitt's waist. 'What can we do for you, Inspector?'

'It's actually Bernard I've come to see.' Inspector Palmer took an envelope from his jacket pocket. 'The bank want to invite him to a little ceremony next weekend so the Manager can say his thank you and present the reward money.'

The bank had offered a five thousand pound reward for information leading to the return of the stolen money and Bernard, as the person who had found the suitcase in the car, had already been told it would be his.

'He's next door with Karen,' said Mrs Hewitt. 'I'll go and get him.' She gave Mr Beasley a quick kiss and disappeared out of the door.

'He's all right, I hope?' Inspector Palmer put his envelope on the hall table. 'Only I heard that, when you got to the hospital that Sunday, his aunt had unfortunately passed away. It must have been rather upsetting.'

'Yes, it was,' Mr Beasley agreed. 'For all of us, but especially Bernard. They were very close, you see. It's not been easy for him, but he's back at school on Monday and we're hoping that'll help take his mind off things.'

'Yes.'

Inspector Palmer hesitated a moment before speaking again. 'I also heard that he had a rather strange experience while he was at the hospital.'

'You mean seeing and talking to his aunt after she . . . yes, well, that was certainly strange all right.' Mr Beasley shook his head. 'Though the staff nurse said it wasn't as uncommon as people think. She'd come across several cases, believe it or not. I suppose if you're a nurse you get to see these things more than . . .' He stopped. Bernard had appeared at the front door.

'Good to see you, Bernard.' Inspector Palmer held out a hand. 'I've come to say thank you again for what you did, and to give you this.' He picked up the envelope and passed it across.

'Thanks,' said Bernard.

'And I thought you might like to know your Mrs Donaldson goes to trial at the end of April, so I don't think she'll be bothering you for a few years after that.' He turned to Mr Beasley. 'Though she's never told us how she did it.'

'She won't talk to you?'

'Oh, she talks. Talks all the time, but all she'll give us is some story about a magic pocket watch, she says belonged to Bernard's aunt.'

'Magic?' Mr Beasley laughed. 'Well, Aunt Bee had a pocket watch all right, but it's the first I've heard of it being magic. She gave it to Bernard.'

'Oh! Did she, now?' Inspector Palmer's mouth was smiling, but his eyes looked carefully at Bernard's face. 'Sounds interesting. Could I see it?'

Bernard took the watch from his pocket.

'It stopped when she died,' he said, as he passed it across. 'It hasn't gone since.'

'Like the grandfather clock, eh?' Inspector Palmer looked carefully at the watch. The hands pointed to exactly one minute to twelve. He reached a thumb to the button at the top and pressed down.

'Well, it doesn't seem to do anything for me.' He pressed the button a couple more times and passed the watch back to Bernard. 'Thank you for letting me see it.' He pointed to the envelope. 'I've put my address and phone number in there, so if there's anything I can do . . .' He was looking closely at Bernard again. 'You know, if you lose a bicycle, or you find an animal that needs looking after, or you know of someone who's being bullied . . . you let me know.'

'Yes, I will,' said Bernard. He returned Inspector Palmer's gaze without blinking. 'Thank you.'

In the back pocket of his trousers, Inspector Palmer had four handwritten notes and it had been his intention, when he first came, to show them to Bernard and ask if he could offer any sort of an explanation. But now he changed his mind.

There were several reasons for this. In the first place, he had the feeling that Bernard had been through a good deal in the last few weeks and deserved a little time to recover. He was also not sure that, if he did produce the notes, they would necessarily have any effect. The boy in front of him had a self-possessed, *solid* look about him, and Inspector Palmer suspected he was quite capable of simply denying that he'd written the notes in the first place.

And the truth was that the policeman could not only not prove anything, but was not sure what it was he wanted to prove. The idea he half had was so ridiculous that trying to prove it might well make him a laughing stock. As a newly promoted Inspector, he had no wish to damage his reputation. If a crime had been committed, he might have been tempted to act, but since the reverse was true, and Bernard had actually helped solve one, Inspector Palmer decided the best thing would be to say nothing.

A part of him would have liked to know the truth, simply to satisfy his curiosity, but good policemen learn very early in their careers to control their curiosity. Instead, he simply handed Bernard back the watch.

'Pity it stopped like that,' he said. 'It'd be rather useful if it was going, wouldn't it?'

'Yes,' Bernard agreed sadly. 'Yes, it would.'

The fact that the watch was not going was something that Bernard and Karen both found deeply frustrating. They had made various attempts to wind it up. There was a tiny hole in the base of the watch, which was the only place that a key might fit, and the children had poked pins, wire and even a compass needle down it, but to no avail.

Mrs Hewitt had suggested they take the watch to a repair shop and Bernard's father said there was a man who restored antique clocks and watches near the wagon depot, but Bernard declined the offer. If someone *did* succeed in winding up the watch, he thought, like Mrs Donaldson, they would almost certainly want to keep it for themselves. Then he would be worse off than ever.

For the moment, presuming that Aunt Bee had made a mistake and that the key was still somewhere in her house, the children had pinned their hopes on a careful search bringing it to light. In her will, she had left the property to Bernard's father to look after until Bernard was twenty-one, so they had a free run of the place during the Easter holidays.

But the search had proved vain. In the mass of furniture, trunks, desks and papers, they had found some highly revealing insights into Aunt Bee's earlier life, including a fighter pilot's log book from 1944, seven separate degrees from Oxford University and a journal entitled *My time in Tibet* – but no key. At least, none the right size. They had found dozens of keys of a great variety of types and shapes, but nothing that would fit the small hexagonal hole at the bottom of the watch.

The more he thought about it, the more Bernard was convinced that he was missing something obvious. It was a feeling that grew with each passing day and he was still brooding over the problem on Monday morning, when Karen met him at the pavement and they set off to school together for the start of the new term.

Karen was thinking about the same problem but, unlike Bernard, she did not brood in silence. She talked about it. She talked a lot these days, in fact Mrs Hewitt said the real problem was getting her to stop. It was as if she was trying to catch up on the words she had missed saying when she was younger.

'The thing that puzzles me,' she was saying, her

cello case dragging along the ground as they turned into the school gates, 'is that, the way you describe it, she was so definite. She told you she'd given you the key. She definitely said that's what she'd done. Why would she say something like that if she hadn't?'

Bernard grunted.

'I suppose she could have been confused.' Karen pushed open the main school doors and led the way inside. 'After all, she was dead when she said it. Did she sound confused to you at all?'

'No.' Bernard shook his head. 'But I *know* she never gave me a key. The only thing she ever gave me was the watch. I can't understand it.'

Miss Picot, looking taller than ever, was passing the coat-room, and her eyes lit up as she saw Bernard.

'Ah! The very person I wanted to see. You had a good holiday, I hope?' Their form mistress did not wait for a reply. 'I've put a list on the board asking anyone who wants to be considered for the cricket team to sign up. Frankly we could do with someone with your ball skills, Bernard. As a fielder? Wicket keeper maybe?'

'That's very kind of you,' said Bernard, 'but I'm not sure I'll have the time for team sports this term.'

'Oh!' Miss Picot's face fell. 'Well, it's up to you, of course, but do think about it. Let me know if you change your mind, eh?'

'That's not entirely true, is it?' said Karen as she and Bernard walked down the corridor to the music room.

'What?'

'When you said the only thing your aunt ever gave you was the watch.' Karen paused in the doorway. 'I mean, if you think about it, she gave you lots of things. There was the bottle of iron tonic. In hospital she gave you the grapes and the chain for your watch. There was the notebook for the moths . . . I know none of them were the key, but maybe if you went over everything you did together . . .'

'Welcome back you two!' Mr Tree was striding towards them on his way to the staffroom. 'I hope you don't mind, but I've put you both in for the maths competition on Thursday.' He beamed at them as he swept past. 'I think with you two on the team, we should wipe the floor with the opposition. OK? Good to see you back!'

Karen watched as he disappeared down the corridor.

'That could be a bit tricky.' She went into the music room and propped her cello in the corner by the piano. 'I mean, if you can't use the watch, you're not going to be able to . . .'

She stopped. Bernard was clearly not listening. He had followed her into the room and was feverishly emptying out his pockets on to a table.

'What is it? What's the matter?'

'The chain.' Bernard had taken out his watch, a handkerchief, several sweets and a pencil sharpener. 'She gave me the chain, didn't she?'

Abandoning his pockets, he had picked up his school bag and tipped it up. In the pile of books, papers and pens, there was the watch chain and, as he held it up, a slow smile spread across his face.

'You see?'

Karen did indeed see. At one end of the chain was the clip that joined it to the ring at the top of the watch, but at the other were the two slender gold rods, hinged in the middle, which went through a button hole. When Bernard opened them, three of the arms of the cross that they made ended in little nodules, like the head of a pin, but the fourth . . . the fourth was a slender hexagonal rod.

'It is, isn't it?' breathed Karen. 'It has to be!'

Bernard picked up the watch from the table and slowly moved the rod towards its base. At the last minute, like a needle moving towards a magnet, it was drawn of its own will into the hole and almost immediately started to turn.

Without Bernard touching it, the key spun round and round . . . thirty, forty, fifty turns and it was still spinning, faster and faster . . . Sixty, seventy, eighty . . . until finally, it spun more slowly and gently . . . and stopped.

The key fell back into Bernard's palm.

When he turned the watch over to look at the face, neither of them was surprised to see the hands were pointing to ten to nine. Exactly the time on the wall clock above the piano.

'Try it,' said Karen. 'Try it and see if it –'

Bernard pressed the button and the world stopped.

Beside him, Karen stared unmoving at the watch

in his hand. The curtains at the window no longer fluttered in the breeze but hung, motionless, in the air. Outside, the children coming down the path were frozen in their tracks. There was not a sound to be heard from anywhere.

He had forgotten how peaceful it was, Bernard thought, as he walked slowly out to the playground. How restful and calming it was to be in a world that was completely silent and still. Above him, the leaves on the trees were motionless, their branches bent in an invisible wind. Over by the fence, Mr Wickerstaffe was pointing at a piece of paper falling to the ground, telling some child to pick it up. And over by the climbing frame, there were sparrows, caught in mid-flight just as there had been the day his aunt first gave him the watch.

A good deal had happened to him since that day, he thought. The football, the maths test, going into hospital, Karen, Mrs Donaldson, his aunt falling ill and . . . So much had happened, yet in an odd way it felt like the beginning of an adventure, rather than the end. He took a deep breath and gazed happily at the scene around him. There were so many things he was going to do now that he had the watch back. So many exciting things!

When he turned to go back into school, he passed Mr Tree, frozen in mid-sentence in the main school corridor, talking to Miss Picot by the noticeboards. On an impulse, Bernard borrowed a pencil from the headmaster's jacket pocket and added his name to the list of people who wanted to play cricket that term. Then he saw another notice next to it, asking if anyone would like to play tennis, and he wrote Karen's name at the top.

Finally, he went back to the music room and pressed the button on the watch.

'. . . still works,' said Karen. 'Go on, try it.'

'I just did,' said Bernard. 'And it's fine. Everything's fine.' Pulling up a chair, he smiled happily as he passed the watch to Karen, who pressed the button and disappeared. An instant later, she was standing the other side of him with a plate of chocolate cake and some crumbs on the side of her mouth.

'That is *so* good!' She sat down in the chair beside Bernard with a contented sigh. 'I'd forgotten how peaceful it all was, you know? How . . . *relaxing*!' She put the watch carefully on the table in front of them and passed him the plate. 'They're doing fudge cake for lunch in the kitchens. You want some? We've got time.'

'Thanks.'

Bernard took the cake, but did not start eating. Instead, the two children sat there, side by side for a while, staring happily at the watch, neither of them saying anything.

Eventually, it was Bernard who broke the silence.

'I was thinking,' he said.

'Yes?'

'If Aunt Bee was right when she said she'd given me the key, she could have been right about the other stuff as well.'

'What other stuff?' asked Karen.

'She said if I was going to use the watch properly, I had to know what it was for. And then she said it was for learning.'

'Learning? Learning what?'

'Yes.' Bernard nodded. 'She said that was the first bit you had to work out.'

'Oh.' Karen thought for a moment. 'Any idea what she meant?'

Bernard shook his head. 'Not really.'

But he was going to find out, he thought. One way or another, he was definitely going to find out. He reached out to take the watch from the table and held it in the palm of his hand.

After all, he had plenty of time. All the time in the world.

Psst!
What's happening?

sneakpreviews@puffin

For all the inside information on the hottest new books,

click on the Puffin

www.puffin.co.uk